THE BULGARIAN TRUCK

DUMITRU TSEPENEAG

THE BULGARIAN TRUCK

A BUILDING SITE BENEATH THE OPEN SKY

TRANSLATED BY ALISTAIR IAN BLYTH

DALKEY ARCHIVE PRESS

LIBRARY OF CONGRESS CATALOGING-IN-PUBLICATION DATA

Tsepeneag, Dumitru, 1937-
[Camionul bulgar. English]
The Bulgarian truck / Dumitru Tsepeneag ; translated by Alistair Ian Blyth. -- First edition.
pages cm
ISBN 978-1-56478-698-2 (pbk. : alk. paper)
1. Novelists--Fiction. 2. Married people--Fiction. I. Blyth, Alistair Ian, translator. II. Title.

PC840.3.E67C3613 2015
859'.334--dc23

201403347

Partially funded by the Illinois Arts Council, a state agency.
This publication is supported in part by an award from the National Endowment for the Arts

www.dalkeyarchive.com

Victoria, TX / McLean / London / Dublin

Dalkey Archive Press publications are, in part, made possible through the support of the University of Houston-Victoria and its programs in creative writing, publishing, and translation.

Typesetting: Mikhail Iliatov
Printed on permanent/durable acid-free paper

TRANSLATOR'S PREFACE

Even in the original, *The Bulgarian Truck* is a novel acutely conscious of its own translatedness. The narrator, who, like the author, is a Romanian émigré writer living in Paris, is still bound to his native language and culture, but knows that if his book is to stand any chance of being read by more than a handful of people on the fringes of Europe, it will have to be translated. But even as a writer in translation, he harbours no illusions as to the extent of his readership:

> in Romania they'll hardly be rushing out to read the book. Or in any other country, for that matter, in France, for example . . . How many readers have I had in France, my adopted homeland? I can count them on my fingers. Or maybe the translations have been to blame.

On the other hand, the narrator knows all too well that the average reader—or rather *le grand public*—is avid for a story, for that which can most readily be translated from the written to the audio-visual medium: 'the kind of literature that is suited to film adaptations,' he calls it. And so, although she is a writer he cannot stand, the narrator grudgingly takes inspiration from Marguerite Duras's film *Le Camion* (1977) and sets about constructing a story involving a Bulgarian truck driver making his way westward across Europe.

The (generic) Bulgarian truck driver also happens to be a French political bogeyman, invented by Philippe Villiers, and thereby lends topicality to the narrator's project for a novel. Press cuttings about nationalist discontent in Bulgaria and Bulgarian truck drivers undercutting their French counterparts are interspersed among the various other textual materials of what the narrator calls his 'building site beneath the open sky.' These include the unpunctuated and progressively oneiric ('in dreams there are no commas') narrative involving Tsvetan, the driver of the eponymous Bulgarian truck, and Beatrice, an erotic dancer, who, being literally impenetrable, as a character undermines the reading public's demand for the inclusion of sex scenes in every novel; passages in which the narrator squabbles with his wife (a character from an earlier novel) over the telephone about the inconsistencies and shortcomings of the text in progress; and an exchange of e-mails with Milena / Mailena, the more successful Slovakian novelist with whom the narrator is having an extra-marital affair, but who ultimately turns out to be yet another textual construct.

In a way, we might also read the Bulgarian truck as a metaphor for east-European literature. Continental literary traffic is mostly one way, from West to East, with hundreds of western writers being translated in the languages of the erstwhile communist bloc annually. But like the ramshackle Bulgarian truck, with its dodgy brakes and uncategorisable, non-standard cargo, a few eastern writers still manage to make the journey in the opposite direction, even if, like Tsvetan, they don't get to compete with the big trucks in the endurance race at Alès.

As an east-European novelist, the narrator writes both to be translated and to avoid translating, which, at the start of the novel, he compares to 'play[ing] the part of Flea the Footman to some great writer or other (let's see how they translate that allusion!).' This parenthetical comment points to the insuperable untranslatability of cultural allusions when they come from 'minor' cultures, whose histories and stories have not entered global circulation, have not been 'carried across.' Who outside Romania knows that Flea the Footman was a diminutive (hence the nickname) fifteenth-century Moldavian page who once famously crouched on the ground so that the heroic but equally pint-sized Stephen the Great could use him as a stool when mounting his horse? In other words, far from standing on the shoulders of giants, the writer clambers on the shoulders of midgets like himself. The translator might of course find an equivalent image to convey this meaning, but at the price of discarding the narrator's resigned meta-textual comment on the impossibility of his original image being carried across into another language. But since *The Bulgarian Truck* is 'a building site beneath the open sky' rather than a novel, all the stages of the textual construction process are exposed to the reader's view, even those that have been deleted, or rather placed *sous rature*.

At a number of points in the text, the narrator announces that he has deleted the sentence or paragraph we have just read. The computer has made the process of writing simpler because it has made the task of deletion simpler. As the narrator observes:

> What I've written so far seems rather humourless. I've been ploughing the sands . . . If I don't delete it, it's because I have all the time in the world to do so. At a single click it will all vanish into nothingness. Nothingness helps us to exist. Which is to say, it helps us not to keep looking for a meaning to existence. Not to keep nit-picking.

The function of the computer is no longer to compute, to calculate, but to arrange and to organise; the writer tapping away at his computer keyboard brings order to his text, adding, expanding, embellishing, inserting, copying, pasting, annihilating where necessary: 'That's why the *ordinateur* was invented! More for deleting than for writing.' It is also for this reason that the narrator insists on using the French *ordinateur* (in Romanian: *ordinator*, rather than the standard *calculator*, which is in any case steadily losing ground to *computer*, a loanword from English): 'I don't like the word *computer*, and not only because it comes from English: I just don't think it's an appropriate word for the tool in question, although maybe it used to be, long ago.' In this context, it is significant that the term *ordinateur*, proposed in 1955 by Latin philologist Jacques Perret, once had a strong religious charge, having been used to describe God bringing order to the world.[1]

1 Antoine Picon, *"Ordinateur/Computer/Numérique/Digital"*, in Barbara Cassin (ed.), Dictionary of *Untranslatables: A Philosophical Lexicon*, Princeton University Press, 2014, p. 628.

The narrator's awareness of the translatedness and (un)translatability of the text he is in the process of writing is not abstract and theoretical, but intimately bound up with real translators in the real world, who are drawn into the fiction, absorbed by it, becoming characters in their own right. The narrator's wife, who is away in New York, but whose cavilling advice on his novel under construction he seeks over the telephone, rails at him for including passages without punctuation, because, she says, they are 'not good': 'Not for anybody! Neither for readers nor for critics. Not to mention the translator . . .' And she should know, because it turns out that she has bumped into Dumitru Tsepeneag's real-life translator, Patrick Camiller, in a bookshop. She only vaguely remembers the title of the book he has translated, however: 'Wasn't he the one who translated *The Something-or-other Wedding*?' Such is her low opinion of her husband's work that she only has a passing acquaintance with it and is not even sure which novels she herself appears in ('"You are in *Hotel Europa*,"' yells the narrator down the telephone in exasperation). The text of *The Bulgarian Truck* is therefore acutely aware of its own translatedness, but also of the fact that translations are contingent upon flesh-and-blood translators. And this is why the illness and finally the death of Alain Paruit, Tsepeneag's French translator, cast an *adumbratio* over the novel. Paruit withdraws ever deeper into his own terminal illness, no longer interested in books or the world of the text, drawn into a fiction he will never translate.

Marianne herself is suffering from a mysterious, oneiric illness and has gone to New York to seek treatment. With the unassailable logic of a dream, she shrinks to the size of a schoolgirl, only then to grow so tall that she ends up too long for the conjugal bed. The illness is in fact an oneiric echo of one of Tsepeneag's earliest short stories, 'Confidențe' (Confidences), published in his first collection of prose, *Exerciții* (Exercises), in 1966.[2] In the story, the narrator bumps into an acquaintance on the street (such chance encounters also play a part in *The Bulgarian Truck*). Together they go to an insalubrious

2 *Exerciții*, Editura Pentru Literatură, Bucharest, 1966.

tavern, where they drink vodka (oneiric echoes of Raskolnikov and Marmeladov). While the waiter stands by, idly picking his nose, the derelict acquaintance recounts how his wife has started growing shorter and then taller, but when he takes the incredulous and increasingly disgusted narrator to his grubby, evil-smelling flat to show her to him, she has disappeared. Similarly, Marianne, a strong presence throughout the first half of the novel, during which she relentlessly hectors and mocks the narrator in regard to the ineptitude of the novel he is struggling to write, slowly fades away and finally disappears. The narrator speaks to her briefly on the telephone, without knowing that it will be the last time, and then she is gone, without a trace.

The two fictional protagonists that the narrator invents—Tsvetan and Beatrice—also spring from texts included in *Exercises*, texts which, their original punctuation having been washed away, now bob to the surface almost five decades later, as if from the depths of a dream. Tsvetan is inserted into the opening paragraphs of 'La vizita medicală,' an oneiric story describing the routine medical examination of pupils at a boys' school. The oneiric element comes in the form of an understated detail at the end of the story, but which subverts the 'reality' of the rest of the text:

> The boy groaned, no longer putting up any resistance, but his fat body quivered like a gelatinous mass. From the child's belly button grew a white rose. The doctor raised his spectacles onto his forehead, cast a brief glance at the nurse, and then, without a word, pulled up the boy's trousers, but with care, covering his belly. The nurse went to the window, leaning her elbows on the sill. She pressed her forehead to the pane. On the pavement, the children were playing hopscotch.[3]

Tsvetan becomes the unnamed lad earlier in the story who cracks a joke about another boy having dirty feet. Similarly, Beatrice becomes one of the children in 'Amintire' (Memory), the first story in the volume *Exercises*, which is set in a park hovering between

3 *Exerciții*, p. 51.

the real and the unreal, haunted by indeterminate, elongated, distorted animals, like those which invade the re-occurring dreamlike marine landscape that foreshadows death throughout *The Bulgarian Truck*.

In *The Bulgarian Truck*, the narrator himself claims not to dream. Casting around for a subject and characters for his novel, he asks his more widely read wife to give him some ideas:

> —Describe a dream . . .
>
> —A dream?
>
> —A dream. Or two dreams, combining them both. What do I know? You're the writer. Or at least so you claim. A writer . . .
>
> —All right, but I don't dream.
>
> (. . .)
>
> —How can you not dream! Everybody dreams. If you don't dream, it means you're abnormal. How then can you have the gall to address normal readers? Readers that dream . . .

This, in essence, was the premise of *oneirism*, a literary and aesthetic movement led by Dumitru Tsepeneag and Leonid Dimov, which emerged in Romania in the late 1960s: the *oneirist* writer does not dream, but rather he lucidly structures his texts according to the logic of the dream. The surrealist, by contrast, describes/transcribes his dreams, mines his dreams for images, even writes while in a deliberately induced dreamlike state. In a theoretical text published in 1968, two years after *Exercises,* Tsepeneag clearly states the difference between *oneirism* and surrealism: 'for oneiric literature as I conceive it, the dream is neither a source nor an object of study; the dream is a *criterion.* The distinction is fundamental: I do not describe a dream (mine or somebody else's), but rather I attempt to construct a reality *analogous* to the dream.'[4] Realities analogous to the dream, whether textual or otherwise, were anathema in the Socialist

4 Dumitru Tsepeneag, 'În căutarea unei definiții' (In search of a definition), *Luceafărul*, nos. 25-28, June–July 1968; in Leonid Dimov and Dumitru Tsepeneag, *Momentul oniric. Antologie* (*The Oneiric Moment. Anthology*), ed. Corin Braga, Cartea Românească, Bucharest, 1997, p. 25.

Republic of Romania, however. *Oneirism*, an unconventional and highly original literary movement that defied po-faced, duplicitous socialist realism (and realism in general), was viewed very dimly indeed by the communist authorities and was finally suppressed during the cultural crackdown that ensued after the publication in 1971 of Ceaușescu's 'July Theses,' which were inspired by the dictator's recent visit to Maoist China, North Korea and Mongolia.

It is from oneiric writer Leonid Dimov (1926–1987) that the epigraph to *The Bulgarian Truck* comes: 'In love, Dimov used to say, you have no choice but to exaggerate. It's the only way you can be sure of getting your message across.' Dimov was a Romanian[5] poet, essayist, and translator—the poets he translated include Giambattista Marino, whose love sonnets are remarkable for their exaggerated *concettismo*. It is also to Dimov that Tsepeneag's first book, *Exercises*, is dedicated, simply: 'To Leonid Dimov.' The epigraph is one of the many intertextual allusions to be found in *The Bulgarian Truck*, allusions both to Tsepeneag's own work, which now spans five decades, and to universal literature. Among the more obvious allusions are Beatrice, who has been transplanted from Paradise to the gates of Hell, and Milena, although unlike Kafka, who wrote letters to her, the more up-to-date narrator writes e-mails. For all its oneiric irruptions and despite the author's humorous pretence that his bumbling narrator is making it up as he goes along, *The Bulgarian Truck* is constructed with consummate logical rigour. With the satisfaction of solving an intricate puzzle, we become aware of the full complexity of the novel's structure as we read its closing pages, when the final pieces of the building site fall into place. But this is what the narrator told us at the very beginning: that he is interested in structure, rather than story. Each of Tsepeneag's novels is

5 In *The Bulgarian Truck*, Milena assumes, judging by his name, that Leonid Dimov must be Russian or Bulgarian. In fact, he was born in Bessarabia, then a province of Greater Romania, subsequently the Soviet Socialist Republic of Moldavia, and now the majority Romanian-speaking Republic of Moldova. The fluidity of east-European identities is a theme of *The Bulgarian Truck*. Milena (or is it Mailena?) oscillates between Czech and Slovak, Prague and Bratislava. Dimov is a Romanian writer with an obviously Slavic name. And as for Tsepeneag, it may ultimately derive from Turkish, or maybe from Hungarian, but nobody is sure.

unique in its structure. Think of the marvellous fugue structure of *Vain Art of the Fugue*, for example. But taken together, they might be said to form an even more complex hyper-structure, in which an entire series of motifs, devices and symbols recur with oneiric insistence. *The Bulgarian Truck* is thus part of a continuum, whose origins lie in 1960s Romania, where, for an all too brief period, one of twentieth-century Europe's most remarkable literary movements arose.

THE BULGARIAN TRUCK

In love, Dimov used to say, you have no choice but to exaggerate. It's the only way you can be sure of getting your message across.

I'm going to write to her, because I simply must tell somebody about it. I want to share with her the new way of composing a novel that I have in mind. Structure is what interests me the most in a novel, but apart from that, to be honest, I don't care about telling a story, even a very interesting, enthralling, sensational story. That kind of thing leaves me cold ... Even as a reader I'm not very interested in the subject, and that's why I rarely read literature. Novels, I mean. I prefer novellas. They're shorter. She knows this very well, and so there's no point in my telling her yet again or, which is more likely, in her contradicting me. She loves contradicting people. No, this isn't why I'm going to write to her, especially given that it's harder for us to quarrel long-distance, for us to contradict each other, to defend our different viewpoints like two intellectuals each convinced of their own ideas and ready to argue for them to the bitter end. There's nothing wrong in that. Especially given that I'm not at all sure that I will succeed: there's no question of my convincing her, but I can't even swear that I'll go the whole way with this vague plan I have in my head: to write another novel that won't be like any of the other ones I've written up to now ...

Marianne is in New York at the moment, and it takes the mail a few days to get there. That's as quick as it can be. So, that means three or four days for the letter to arrive, and then another two days before she deigns to reply ... Sometimes it doesn't take her more than a few hours. She writes quickly, and she thinks quickly, not to mention that she gets angry quickly because she loses her temper over about anything. Of course, her temper tantrums are a pose. She's spoiled and knows she can get her own way. You might even say I'm the one who is to blame for always having let her get her own way . . . All the same, I think that ever since she was little, ever since childhood, when her parents probably pampered her (she was an only child!) and put up with all her caprices—ever since childhood, as I was saying, she's been accustomed to being flighty and demanding at the same time. How do I know this? Well, if I didn't know, who else do you think would know?

Anyway, I won't get her reply for seven or eight weeks from now, and that's being optimistic. And then what will I do? If I wait that long, I'll lose my urge to write, and then I'll start playing chess instead or, worse still, I'll start translating something, I'll play the part of Flea the Footman to some great writer or other (let's see how they translate that allusion!); I'm not saying I don't like that: I love to translate, to luxuriate in two languages that I can speak almost equally well, but translation, whatever they might say, is a waste of time for a writer, and at my age I'll end up bitterly regretting any waste of time, in the final moments before I commit suicide or when I'm confined to a wheelchair without either the will or the strength to kill myself . . .

'You've gone crazy,' Marianne would shout if she could read my mind, if she could observe everything passing through my head as I sit stupefied here in front of the computer, carrying on this monologue instead of writing. Especially given I have no excuse whatsoever. Nowadays, thanks to the computer, we are no longer able to talk to the paralysing whiteness of a sheet of paper. We can no longer complain . . . And so, I ought to make an effort to write, to write anything, as long as I can say that I'm writing, that my fingertips are tapping the keyboard of the *ordinateur* (I don't like the word *computer*, and not only because it comes from English: I just don't think it's an appropriate word for the tool in question, although maybe it used to be, long ago . . .). Whatever happens, something will still crop up on the vaguely white square in front of me.

All right, here is what I'm going to do: I'm going to create a monologue, tapping away at the keyboard of the *ordinateur*.

Agreed, it's not an e-mail I'm writing, because Marianne doesn't have an *ordinateur* where she is, nor is it even a letter.

I should say that my printer is broken and therefore I couldn't even pretend that I'm writing her a letter. There wouldn't be any point. What I mean is that despite appearances, I have no intention of fooling anybody.

And certainly not her.

a monologue is different from a letter I don't have to wear myself out with punctuation and even as far as spelling goes there's a lot more leeway especially when it comes to Tsvetan the truck driver who gave the impression of never having got further than primary school whereas in fact he had been to high school although it was all like water off a duck's back to him apart from that he is deft and intelligent he speaks sparingly but well especially to the ladies who are obviously attracted to him and how could they not be attracted to him have you seen his biceps his pectorals his shoulders his dark eyes and his greasy skintight trousers external signals granted but what else do you expect poor women to go by there's always a risk you might be mistaken and end up with a pansy in any case when they have a bit of experience women are almost always right on target especially if they sense that the male doesn't waver goes in straight for the kill knows the ancient code which hasn't changed much

but if this is what it's going to be like then the whole novel can be taken as a monologue that only comes to an end because the author gets it into his head to publish it to see his name on the cover it's for his own satisfaction I can well understand when you're starting out I mean starting out on a career but after that I wonder whether it can still be called a *satisfaction* we might sooner talk about an obligation although to whom is not at all apparent

Dear M.,

I have started writing The Bulgarian Truck, *half of whose title is lifted from your favourite writer, the one I can't abide. Between her and me there is a huge gulf. Let me explain why. According to the latest socio-psychological research, there are two major differences within the human species: sex difference and age difference. (If you want details, one of the ones to read is Dany-Robert Dufour; he is published by Denoël.) Death widens the gulf even more (I'm thinking of the implacable maxim of the encyclopaedias!); for although the two differences accumulate in parallel, as long as the individuals are alive, we cannot exclude the possibility, at least in theory, of copulation occurring between them, as a result of which it may be hoped that these differences might temporarily and to a certain extent be reduced.*

Marguerite Duras was attracted to younger men, even men much younger than herself. She was a real 'cougar' . . . And so for quite a while I was unable to stop myself thinking about an eventuality that I found not only undesirable, but also repellent: that she might also be attracted to me. I admit I was slightly wide of the mark. By the time I arrived in France, the novelist was already old, and in any case too old for my taste. I had seen a photograph of her taken by an American photographer in which she looked like a bag lady: she was squat, with broomstick legs, and her large head, plonked on top of her body, was made to look even larger by an enormous cake-shaped hairdo. Do you remember? We were a couple by then. One night I dreamed that she was groping me, her hands were clamped to my belt like a witch's claws, and she was desperately trying to pull my trousers down. In that nightmare of mine, I thought, what the hell, why not let her? If she manages to bring me to the state of arousal required for copulation, then all well and good, she'll deserve it . . . And if not, then maybe she will calm down. You told me the same thing, laughing your head off, when I recounted the dream: let her, it won't kill you! Afterwards, we made love, for a long while, until we fell flat on our backs, our strength drained . . .

I think this is also the reason I wasn't able to read her novels, and you would get annoyed and treat me in a deplorable way, especially when you heard me scornfully remark that I found them pretentious: strained populism, I used to say. I was referring to her early novels in particular. But also to The Lover. *All right, I know, the later stuff, particularly her plays, a few films . . .* The Truck, *yes, of course . . .*

'You haven't got a clue about French literature!' you used to upbraid me. And even less of a clue about English-speaking literature, the great literature of our times. And you would reel off a

list of names, some of which I had never heard of, some of which I had seen on book covers in bookshops, although I hadn't read their books. I would flick through them, read a few lines, and then put them back on the shelf or the counter.

I think you were right. I'm still what I was then: a peasant from the Danube . . .

And you added: the only writer from the East who has got the slightest idea is Milan Kundera. You would do better to ponder the profound definition the Czech novelist gives: 'The art of the novel is the art of complexity.'

What can I say? It's profound. It's certainly profound . . .

What I've written so far seems rather humourless. I've been ploughing the sands . . . If I don't delete it, it's because I have all the time in the world to do so. At a single click it will all vanish into nothingness. Nothingness helps us to exist. Which is to say, it helps us not to keep looking for a meaning to existence. Not to keep nit-picking.

I look out of the window: the sky is grey, but it isn't raining . . . It's not cold enough for snow. We're in Paris after all: it snowed for a few days last month and the result was huge traffic jams. Not being used to the snow, Parisians were panicked. I wonder what they would do if they were exiled to Siberia. I'm joking, of course . . . Or what they will do when the famous Gulfstream vanishes. This time I'm not joking: it looks like a very real possibility, a seemingly paradoxical consequence of global warming.

I'm not as profound as Kundera, which doesn't mean I shouldn't make efforts to better myself: to dig as deeply as I can . . . Where? Into the text, where else . . . Writing is like a building site beneath the open sky (I can almost picture you shaking your head). And I shouldn't hesitate to delete, I shouldn't be too lazy to perform such pencil-pusher labours: to write, to delete, and to delete again . . . That's why the ordinateur *was invented! More for deleting than for writing . . . I don't even need to delete everything. What I mean to say is, only the things I don't like or I imagine others might not like, those others who will make the effort to read what I write.*

The reader ought to be able to delete the things he doesn't like. To choose. To construct a book to his own taste using a writer's sentences and words . . . Although for this to happen, books would have to circulate on the internet. But not in their final form. Provisory texts

... Open texts ... Be they only books by authors who have agreed to play the game: let the readers have a say, let them delete or make additions ... After they have made their modifications and once they are satisfied with them, let them put the text back in circulation, also on the internet, obviously, and thereby let them give other internet users the opportunity to intervene, with the attendant risk that countless versions of the same text might spring up, the same as happens in folklore, when a story or ballad is passed down by word of mouth. Nobody knows where it came from, who originated it, and it spreads throughout a region where the same language is spoken. Or even different languages. That was also a possibility: collective, oral authorship, and likewise oral translation ...

Writers who don't want to join in the game will just have to go on sending their manuscripts to publishers so they can have them printed on paper ... So they can have them published, distributed. Because anyway, people are still not going to rush to the bookshop to buy them. There are going to be fewer and fewer bookshops.

I don't have a television set anymore. I gave it up when I realised that I risked spending more time watching football matches than sitting at my desk, whether in front of the *ordinateur* or not. But even so, I still buy a newspaper or a magazine from time to time. This is how I found out that there is going to be a truck race in Alès that will last the whole weekend; does that mean day and night? There will probably be co-drivers, if not multiple drivers, who will take turns at the wheel.

The ecologists will be thrilled ...

she was looking out of the window

at the bottom of the meadow in front of the house there ran a brook in the last few days it had been raining and so the water had risen it was rather higher than usual higher of course than during droughts when the water trickled dry or was barely visible masked by the vegetation which only just held out against the scorching heat it squeezed its way between the rocks and boulders Beatrice would then run down to the brook to look for snails all she found were their shells the snails had already perished from the heat but she gathered them all the same she would arrange them by size in her room her parents threw them out every now and then without her noticing

she went out of the house barefoot her mother had gone off on the bicycle to do the shopping the grass was wet the little girl headed towards the old plane tree she liked trees that had hollows it was there that she had found the hedgehog a few days before which she had taken back to her room she was inseparable from it in the evening at bedtime she put it to bed

you'll prick yourself on its spines shrieked her mother or Victor if he was at home

when she woke up in the morning she couldn't find the hedgehog she wept she refused to eat

where is the hedgehog

never mind you'll find another one there are hedgehogs all over the place

Victor made her a little wooden house for hedgehogs and so every morning she would search beneath the trees or in the bushes which scratched her mercilessly

Now I really am going to write her a letter, a proper one, which I shall send by post, with a stamp, a postmark, the whole works. I picked up my printer from the repair shop, it looks as good as new, and so I don't have any more excuses. Then, I will take the letter to the post office and hand it to the clerk at the counter, who will put postage on it. I will see her stamp it and then, with a gesture she has probably made thousands of times, toss it in the bin full of other letters waiting to be sent.

I am not going to put it in the post box on the corner of the street because I'm not one hundred percent sure that the postman who comes to collect the letters won't inadvertently drop it, it has been known to happen after all, then pick it up and absentmindedly put it in his pocket. Absentmindedly or intentionally. I read somewhere that there are postmen who steal letters. Yes, yes, they take them home and read them. They don't read anything else, books or newspapers, they read only letters, sometimes they keep them, they collect them, otherwise, if they don't find them interesting, they reseal them and send them to the address on the envelope. I can't take that risk . . .

Dear Marianne,
I miss you. You don't know how much I miss you. I also miss my conversations with you. Especially now that I've restarted writing the novel I've been dragging around after me for so long. The great big truck! . . . In the meantime, it has fallen into complete disrepair. I don't even know whether it's in working order anymore. The sound of the engine is nothing more than the fainter and fainter buzz of a bumblebee caught on a strip of flypaper. (I delete that . . .) *It's missing a wheel, or a tyre, to be more precise. The handbrake doesn't engage, and I can't check the other brake, because I don't dare start the engine. It's a good job my truck is stationary. If I repaired it and bought a brand-new tyre for one of the rear wheels, if I set it in motion, in other words, I'm very afraid that after that I wouldn't be able to bring it to a stop. So, what am I to do? How do I get out of this mess? I have to confess that I don't know, I'm not sure I know how to drive so large a truck, and a rather ramshackle one at that, in any case a rather rusty one given how long it's been in the garage.* (I delete that too.)

You see, this is why I need you, to talk to you . . . about the truck, to ramble on to you, improvising shamelessly, and you to take me to task, because it doesn't take much for you to realise that I'm just beating around the bush and I don't yet have a novel in progress; I'm not counting the beginnings of chapters, the disparate scenes that I need to put together as part of a reasonably coherent text, the notes scribbled on scraps of paper, which most of the time I mislay or just plain lose. And so, as you have guessed, I'm talking to you about a novel that I'm merely thinking of writing, which I really must write, and as soon as possible. The plan of a novel . . . I'm dragging the plan of a novel around after me. And the few pages I scribbled one summer in the country. Which I think I ought to discard, because I don't like them or rather they don't fit the life I'm leading at the moment. My life has changed since you left . . .

I know you find it hard to put up with all this carelessness and untidiness on the part of a scribbler who's never satisfied with what comes out of his pen, dreaming of everything in the moon and stars and foolishly hoping that what he has not yet written might stand a chance of being a masterpiece. But you are an intelligent and generous woman. That's why I need you, your lucidity and energy, your put-

downs that prevent me from wandering too far away from the subject, in fact no, it would be better to say the object, the object of the discussion, I mean to say the letter . . .

Am I a flatterer? Ultimately, why wouldn't I be . . . Why shouldn't I be a flatterer? An ocean stands between us right now, and so perhaps politeness isn't enough. In love, Dimov used to say, you have no choice but to exaggerate. It's the only way you can be sure of getting your message across.

The novel, as I have perhaps told you before, will be called The Bulgarian Truck. *In fact, it's not even a question of a novel. Which is to say, what I am writing can't be called a novel . . . But what then? I've no idea . . .*

Of course I have heard of it, how could I not have heard of the Marguerite Duras film you are so keen on. Lately, I too have started thinking seriously about how it's about time I read her books. I'm not joking. She's a very important author, I beg your pardon, authoress *of French literature, not to mention the fact that for women in this rather reactionary country she was a role model and an incentive to emancipation. Without her there wouldn't have been any Christine Angot, any Camille Laurens, any of the other highly talented authoresses. And that would have been a pity . . . I almost forgot to mention Justine Lévy: just today I read an article about her in the* Journal de Dimanche *by a well-known literary journalist, Laure Delorme or whatever her name is. To cut a long story short, French literature is in good hands! Our country has a golden future . . .*

Don't get angry if every now and then I can't help myself . . . They're innocent wisecracks. I hope you won't get annoyed over so little. And if you are annoyed, then from now on I apologise.

In any event, you're perfectly right when you say that nowadays literature is written mainly by women, as men are no longer capable of feeling any passion for a field that is showing such obvious signs of exhaustion. So, it's no longer profitable from any point of view: neither the glory, nor the money (true, there are still best-sellers, but to do that it's not enough to write to the public taste, you also have to have a little luck). That's what men are like, if it's no longer profitable . . . With a feeling of gratuitousness or out of a fierce but absurd desire to make a living out of their work (for just a few more years), I and a handful of others are among the few still trying to find work in this busy stockyard increasingly dominated by women.

In the old days they used to talk about art for art's sake, now it has fallen to us to talk about art at any cost . . .

You say: it's women who read, and also women who write, while men read the free newspapers they hand out at the exit in the Metro. Newspapers funded entirely by advertising, wretched vehicles for advertisements. I don't read very much, it's true, that is, I don't read novels, but rather poetry, philosophy, and other assorted cheeses, and if I do carry on writing nevertheless, it is because I don't really know how to do anything else. And also so as to please you, my love . . .

I delete that last sentence. I also delete the passage where I talk about flattery and how love's message can't get communicated without exaggeration. Maybe I'll use it as an epigraph, just after the title page. But there's no point in hurrying. I've got all the time in the world. And so I cancel the deletion and the words of Dimov reappear as if by magic. Long live the *ordinateur*! Without it I'd have to write by hand, on ruled paper, I'd have to erase, correct, write it out again, add a word here and there, or a number of words, entire sentences, and then copy it out again, reread it and, if necessary, make further changes. When I remember the typewriter, I can't understand how I had so much patience. What's more, I couldn't type very fast. I used to waste a lot of time. And sometimes, there were so many crossings-out that I would be forced to recopy everything I had written.

True, back then I didn't have to grope my way along, I didn't go round in circles, I knew what I wanted to say, that is, what I wanted to write, or at least I thought I knew . . . I was able to concentrate. And I went straight to the target.

What if I were to delete everything and start all over again?

There are a few scenes I wrote a while back, that I'm fond of, and so I could insert them into all the verbosity up to here. And I have all the time in the world to erase it.

along the lane there stood benches on stumpy lizard legs and the kind of chairs with high-back armrests and curved iron bars by way of legs leafless trees the slender quivering branches traced against a boundless greyish white sky here and there a broad expanse of cropped motionless grass where animals arched elongated bodies around the mane of droplets flowing from the basin of the fountain there were birds with long legs that looked like ostriches but also peacocks they had long silky highly colourful tails all in the gentle and rather sad pale gold light of an autumn Sunday afternoon on the benches old ladies with stiff spindly legs with contorted shoes men with grey or black hats reading the newspaper or just sitting motionless with their eyes on the meadows where those strange animals with fish-bodies and pig-heads were undulating

the gravel of the paths consisting of white and green chips crunched beneath the tiny footfalls of the children that were running to and fro

Beatrice was standing motionless behind a bench she was sulking her hands clenched the wooden back she didn't feel like playing with the other children she liked it in the country not in the city park

it wasn't the same thing

Writing is like a mute, hesitating monologue, a monologue that keeps stopping.

You talk to an audience . . .

Do you talk to somebody or do you talk to yourself?

(Maybe the above thought is one of Kundera's too. I no longer know, but in the end it's of no importance, ideas are like sparrows.)

the asphalt swishes under the wheels of the bicycle he's pedalling carefully with his legs splayed wide so as not to hit his knees against the handlebars he's outgrown the bicycle it makes no difference that he's raised the saddle as far as it will go his aunt bought him it a few years ago it didn't take him long to learn how to pedal it auntie Sonia was proud of him

he sways in the saddle moves from side to side like he's seen the professional cyclists do on television now he's riding in a zigzag and snarling up the traffic the drivers swear at him the cops blow their whistles at him they all curse him or laugh at him and so he decides to avoid the busy roads the crowded boulevards packed with all kinds of vehicles he opts for the quiet streets near the edge of town but unfortunately not all of them are surfaced and then what can he do on the stony not-always-even roadway it's even more difficult the bicycle judders from every joint his knees knock against the handlebars above all one knee keeps hitting the screw that attaches the bell his kneecap is covered in bruises

nicest of all is in the neighbourhood of villas which is the best kept in Sofia here there are few cars and in any event there are no trucks no buses the streets are all asphalted without any cracks or in any event the potholes aren't very big the wheels glide along swishing pleasantly it's a delight to hear them

there aren't very many cars and so the children from the neighbourhood come out to play in the street on the pavement there are lots of them especially during the holidays with balls with bicycles with all kinds of weapons harmless ones obviously but annoying they chase after him on their bicycles they block his path they hurl insults at him they threaten him they poke him with their swords they shoot their bows and arrows at him their catapults sometimes they set their dogs on him

and then what can he do

where can he go

maybe the only solution would be to ride mainly at night until morning until daybreak at night he could even venture to pedal through the centre of town without any great risk

but what would auntie Sonia say she'd get worried she'd panic and call the police look at the time he still hasn't come home the policeman gives a knowing laugh how old is he

he pedals carefully so as not to bang his knees on the handlebars he keeps his legs splayed wide he pedals grimly with a fury that might seem inexplicable he would like to go faster but the bicycle is too small it's old it won't pick up speed all he manages to do is knock his knees against the handlebars he grinds his teeth he swears but all in vain a car comes up behind him overtakes him as quick as a flash he cranes his neck around so far that he almost loses his balance he yanks the handlebars to the right to the left and to the right again and to the left again he pedals even more grimly almost with hatred here's another car then another

we live in the century of speed auntie Sonia

to hell with the century we live in

auntie Sonia was short in stature and very lively like a water bird a lapwing her hair was always black her lips discreetly rouged her cheekbones lightly misted a rosy colour

why do you dye your hair auntie Sonia

I dye so you can ask me why I dye it

why don't you want to try not dyeing it just once so we can see what it'll look like

grey that's what it'll look like

then dye it silver or white as milk or better still light blue don't you want to

shut your mouth you old donkey

I love you

and I love you too even though you've grown up to be a cheeky hobbledehoy

one day he told her that he wanted to become a driver that if he could learn to ride a bicycle he could learn to drive cars trucks he would like to become a driver

a driver

yes a driver

If Marianne were to read what I have written so far, I don't think she'd hesitate to say that she has read all these things before, probably also written by me (here I could exult: aha, so you recognise my style!), and that all I'm doing is repeating myself. For her it's a real obsession: I beat around the bush, it's inexcusable. For, everything has a limit, even repetition . . .

And what could I say back to her? Should I give her the theory of the matchstick, as she likes to call it, should I explain to her that I need these repetitions, which doesn't necessarily mean I'm feeding on myself—Hodja tore chunks out of himself! (the translator can leave out that last bit, which is in fact a quotation from a brilliant poet who is unknown outside the borders of his native land)—and that in any event there is no point in her playing the detective. But then why do I send her my writing to read, why do I keep her from her American and French novels, from that carefully, skilfully formulated literature that is to the taste of the readers it is aimed at? A literature meant to please as many people as possible. A literature of democracy, yes, of our capitalist democracy in its terminal phase. And this literature is taught! There are even schools where future writers study the art of narrative, of dialogue, of suspense. Once you've finished school, you've learned to write, you're a writer: good or bad, but a writer all the same, able to step out in front of Le Grand Public. I don't know whether they also give you a diploma or just a course certificate that you can show to publishers . . .

Poor you, it's obvious you didn't attend any school! Marianne would jeer. And that would shut me up, because she'd be right. It would be pointless to get annoyed or offended at her sneering tone of voice, I wouldn't have any comeback, that is, instead of giving her a sharp, snappy reply, I would be forced to give her a long, tedious theory. I've probably done so before but to no purpose. Marianne is more merciless than the public because she (poor her!) reads me . . .

The best thing to do is not to take any notice of comments of that kind, no matter who makes them.

she slowly carefully opens the door that gives onto the hall she crosses the threshold looking all around her then she creeps across the thick carpet that muffles her footfalls up to the armchair and there she rests her chin on the upholstered back

she smiles lifting her eyes to the painting hanging on the wall

a garden in bloom with benches and multi-coloured birds among the tall flowers the sky is blue tending to violet and the sun casts its rays from somewhere in the background of the painting

she plucks up courage and softly treading with her knees bent and her arms spread she moves from the armchair to the massive chest of drawers in which wolf's eyes sometimes gleam she stops and turns her head towards the window where a chink of grey sky is visible and the roof of the neighbouring tenement block covered in satellite dishes and wires adieu meadow adieu hedgehogs hiding among the leaves

then she half-opens another door and looks through the crack there is no danger they are all asleep Victor is wearing his glasses and his newspaper covers his head like a tent he is snoring softly Beatrice smiles they are all asleep as if enchanted mother and the canary in the cage and the cat curled up on a chair she closes the door her footfalls are more determined nimbler she goes into the dining room on the dark oval table in the black fruit bowl with rusty yellow leaves the bird

red as a flame motionless it is sleeping there peacefully in the rays of sunlight that filter through the window through the curtains it is as big as a blackbird perhaps bigger it has a sharp bluish-grey glossy beak towards the tail the plumage turns orange probably also because of the sun by the opposite wall a sofa covered in cherry-red felt on the sideboard another bird also red but smaller surrounded by all kinds of knickknacks including a very nice pink piglet the chairs around the table have short legs but very high backs they look like horsemen with shakos armour and saddle blankets

she sets her foot as if on a ladder the horse is perhaps beneath the table in any event a white one and from the chair noiselessly raising herself by her elbows up onto the table the bird is still sleeping peacefully it does not feel anything sense anything it is asleep

she moves her arms clasps her elbows at her chest hesitates looks at the sideboard a ray of sunlight gilds the stemmed glasses on the top shelf between the glasses run small multicoloured birds and behind the glasses is a garden with flowering fruit trees and gleaming green grass

now she seems to remember

she has the feeling that old scenes return to her mind

she remembers but she doesn't know what

she looks carefully at the bird in the fruit bowl and she decides with both hands she softly grasps the bird beneath the belly she lifts it from its nest painted with rusty yellow flowers raises it to her lips it is dear to her it has a small head a comically small head and look it has opened one glossy round eye the bird is trembling its body is warm and frightened Beatrice too is overcome with emotion her hands tremble she puts it back in the fruit bowl she almost drops the bird it takes fright it wriggles having come to its senses it spreads its wings it has greenish blackish yellowish legs with dry corrugated skin

it takes flight

with one wing it bumps into the lightshade the amber tassels of the lightshade rustle it flies along the walls seeking an egress and she watches open-mouthed she likes it but she is also afraid outside the light is lower in the sky it is heavier oily a blaze the bird flies around the lightshade into the vitrine among the stemmed crystal glasses the little multicoloured birds there have also taken flight the light is fiercer and fiercer a dwarf sun somewhere in the background casts its ever-fiercer rays

now she remembers

she went there she can't remember when

the flowering fruit trees blaze the birds fly faster and faster and at a given point Beatrice knows for sure that the bird whirling like a flame around the dining room will glimpse the garden with glasses and flowers the garden from childhood with hedgehogs and snails by the stream that ran dry every summer although the grass was still moist beneath the old plane tree to which she used to run barefoot

thither it will fly smaller and smaller beyond the glass of the vitrine

free

the nurse had large breasts and a robe damp at the armpits the pupils from the third form had all come out and the pupils from the second form were taking off their sweaty shirts shoving each other roughhousing and then the doctor raised his eyes from the register and in a calm voice demanded silence when he was talking his grey moustache quivered his sweaty bald patch gleamed but he had a gentle even voice and the din subsided the nurse came to the table her short robe revealed her knees she shouted silence then the names of the first boys in the register Abagian had grown he was almost as tall as the nurse he placed his large close-cropped bonce beneath the horizontal measuring rod why didn't you take off your sandals asked the nurse and slapped the chubby white back that was covered in freckles or maybe they were moles his feet are dirty came the hoarse voice of Tsvetan and then laughter the lad folded his arms across his chest and remained stock-still as if they weren't even talking about him he was gazing out the window at the roof of the building opposite a male pigeon was trying to seduce a female pigeon

they looked the same age

Here is a possibility I hadn't thought of: Marianne receives the letter, picks up the telephone, and calls me.

—What's with this letter? What is it you want from me? If you're in need of some advice, like you say, then don't start theorising about literature, don't start going on at me about such paltry things . . .

I say nothing, I have no answer, although I understand her very well and even think she's probably right.

—Do you hear me?

—Yes, I hear you . . .

—Then why are you playing dumb?

—I'm not playing dumb. I just don't know what to say . . .

—First of all tell me what the novel is about, talk to me about the characters. And above all else, who is driving the truck?

—A Bulgarian truck driver.

—Well then say so. A Bulgarian truck driver transporting goods to Europe.

—But Bulgaria is already in Europe . . .

—Fine, fine . . . Bulgaria, Romania, they're in Europe and yet they're not in Europe. It doesn't really matter.

—Yes it does. Besides, you find out that the truck driver is Bulgarian just from reading the title.

—Are you trying to pick a quarrel with me? Tell me! Is that what you want?

—No, I don't. How could I possibly want to . . .

—And who else is in the truck?

—Nobody. Who else could there be?

—A gypsy stowaway. How should I know?

—No, on my word of honour. Otherwise I would have told you . . . At one point he picks up a little old woman and drops her off fifteen or twenty kilometres further down the road, he gives her a lift from her village to the next village, where her daughter lives. She's married to the village butcher . . . She's fallen ill.

—So . . . Go on.

—This happens in Bulgaria. The truck hasn't crossed the border into Macedonia yet. Her husband has been beating her, threshing her like beans, and she has been screaming and wailing at the top of her voice. All the neighbours hear it. And so one of them tells the old woman when they meet on market day. One of these days that butcher is going to kill her, so she says.

—Passionate!

—You wheedled it out of me. I wouldn't have even talked about it.

—And what goods is the truck transporting?

—I don't know . . .

—How can you not know? You have to know. It's important. Anyway, tell me about the truck driver. How old is he?

—Is it important?

—Would you listen to him! Of course it's important. Does he have a wife, children?

—No, he doesn't. That is, he had a wife, but they're separated. I don't know whether they're divorced. His wife ran off to Sofia.

—To Sofia?

—Where she met a Romanian and went back to Giurgiu with him.

—To Giurgiu?

—She is half-Romanian on her mother's side. Her mother was from near the Danube. She also speaks the language a little.

—What language?

—The Romanian language . . . Her mother was from Zimnicea . . .

—From where?

—From Zimnicea. It's a small town on the Romanian bank of the Danube. Like Giurgiu, except smaller . . .

—How old did you say he was?

—Who, the truck driver?

—Yes, isn't he the main character?

—Yes and no.

—What do you mean?

—There are other characters, too. First of all there is the narrator, who is also the author, as well as being a character himself, which is to say, the other characters talk about him and involve him in the plot. After that . . .

—Off you go again.

—All right, but the author is important, especially if he is also the narrator, as well as being a character. It allows me to make him look omniscient without interfering with the lifelikeness of the plot all that much.

—Rubbish! Tell me what the subject matter is. I want to know what happens. That's what I want to know . . .

—What do you expect to happen? I don't really know. I've only written thirty pages so far.

—Are you going to tell me what happens next or not?

—No . . .

—You don't even know what happens at the end? You haven't got an ending . . .

—I know how I would like it to end, but I don't know how I'm going to get there yet.

—You mean to say that you're writing without knowing what it is you're writing about, without having any idea about how the characters develop and interact. In short, you don't know the plot or the subject of the novel. I can't believe it . . .

—Believe what you like. I am . . . That is, I am not . . .

—I've no idea what you are or what you imagine yourself to be, but whatever you are, you're not a novelist . . .

Marianne angrily hangs up the telephone.

She must have been reading Nicolae Manolescu's *Critical History of Romanian Literature*, I say to myself.

in the morning she would take off her nightgown and stand naked in front of the mirror she had been doing it since she was little she lifted her arms she stretched as far as she could she stood on tiptoes she twisted from left to right she swung twice three times or until she felt dizzy she leaned her chest forward her pre-adolescent budding breasts she raised one leg pointing it backwards to keep her balance she stretched her two arms towards the mirror of course Beatrice did not so much as smile

cavorting like that in front of the mirror she noticed that hair had sprouted on her pubis

I read an article in the newspaper written by Tony Blair, the former British prime-minister, a rather optimistic article: he believes that by 2020 it will be possible to reduce carbon dioxide, if not by one hundred percent, than at least by seventy percent, provided that investments are made in the following three areas: increasing energy efficiency, reducing the rate of deforestation, and harnessing sources of energy with low carbon emissions.

This doesn't prevent him from pointing out that India and China, in their drive to industrialise, will continue to construct carbon-burning power stations: 'To pull hundreds of millions of people out of poverty,' he stresses.

The British prime-minister's rather foolish optimism was also on display during the war in Iraq. And the fact that he was a loyal friend of Bush speaks even less in his favour.

It doesn't even enter his head that the real solutions, probably the only solutions, will be decreased production and strict birth control. How would it be possible to impose such solutions? Very simply: through dictatorship. The word has a bad reputation, it strikes fear . . . Out of pure demagogy, and without having the patience or courage to think about it more deeply, there will be many people who will objurgate me. But they ought at least make the effort to understand that it wouldn't be a utopian socio-economic dictatorship, but one to save the human species. I'm convinced that such a dictatorship is easier to accept and therefore easier to put up with. When a ship is sinking, it's not every man for himself. Discipline is required precisely in order to prevent panic as far as possible. But if we have to wait for it to start to sink . . . Therein lies the whole difficulty: with the naked eye, we can't see the looming catastrophe. When the passengers on the Titanic clapped eyes on the iceberg, it was already too late.

We have to put our trust in the scientists, in their measurements and calculations, no matter how abstract they might be. But there are many more people who believe in priests, rabbis and imams than in the scientists' warnings. Not to mention the obscene, irresponsible demagogy of politicians who can't see farther than today or their own immediate interests.

And another thing: ideas to do with ecology, with global warming and all its effects, are, in my opinion, poorly explained, and they are communicated in completely ridiculous ways. When I hear people going on about how we have to save the planet, I burst out laughing. The planet is in far less danger than the idiotic human species. We might even think that by getting rid of humans (Homo sapiens!), the planet will be much better off than when it was dominated by this vain and whimsical animal.

then they moved on to the next street it was hot the picks and shovels weighed heavier and heavier and the air was heavy stifling it burdened the tops of their heads their backs their shoulders they lugged it along with the sun with the picks and shovels one of them came to a stop and struck the pavement with his pick leaning on it resting on it like a walking stick then he looked all around

this was where they were going to dig

across the road was a bookshop the doors were open the booksellers standing there drowsy from the torrid heat it was seldom that a customer entered at that hour of the afternoon on working days

stripped to the waist the bodies of the diggers glistened with sweat their muscles tensed painfully but rhythmically the picks grimly struck the heat-softened asphalt chunks of road loosened and broke away the noise carried far off throughout the neighbourhood people had got used to the noise of the road works nobody complained although nobody knew exactly why all that digging was going on why it lasted from dawn to dusk

from the shop emerged a bookseller drawn by the pickaxe blows on the pavement opposite he was fat he was holding a ballpoint pen or a fountain pen he kept tapping it on his fingers he looked puzzled he shrugged shook his head behind him gathered a couple of passersby they had stopped as if expecting something

beneath the asphalt the earth was sandy the diggers no longer needed picks they straightened their backs they grasped their shovels with a fierce determination that was incomprehensible to the booksellers over the road

why are they digging

when Beatrice arrived the hole was already quite deep and it was also increasing in length becoming a ditch two of the diggers had jumped down inside only the one that remained outside saw the girl but he did not pay any attention she was holding the handle of a kind of basket it was hard to tell what it contained she came to a stop on the pavement next to them and looked at them curiously that morning she had gone to buy milk and seen them on a different street striking the earth just as furiously maybe they were not the same ones the whole neighbourhood was being dug up she took the milk home and went back out and saw them again but this time she stopped they were tall strong the sweat trickled down their broad sunburnt backs to form rivulets behind them they left deep holes or ditches in which the children played soldiers they also found worms there some as thick as your finger or even thicker and longer they were almost like little snakes they wriggled as they tried to escape from their hands

Beatrice stared in puzzlement her head lolling on one side resting on her upraised left shoulder she had wearied of looking and she couldn't understand why she stayed there rooted to the spot why she kept on gawping idly she moved the basket from one hand to the other and she couldn't really understand what was happening the mound of earth was now growing seemingly higher than the other mounds the diggers did not exchange a word they did not allow themselves to pause for one minute in the hole all that could be seen now was the sunburnt tops of their heads

why all this digging

the booksellers went back into the shop in annoyance the children left too promising to come back in the evening that hole would be bigger than all the others they said among themselves but why are they digging what are they looking for they're looking for the dragon

the gigantic snake coiled beneath the city

Beatrice shuddered as she gazed at the massive back the brawny hairy arms leaning on the spade and the heat enveloped her in a silky blouse she ought to leave so as not to get into an argument at home Victor was ill and he was waiting for her she thought of him with pity but she did not budge her legs had turned to lead and her entire being was slowly slowly drooping melting

the men in the hole were no longer visible the man at the top cast them a stern glance from below his bushy eyebrows then turning round he signalled to the men at the bottom Beatrice couldn't make out what he was saying it was as if he were talking in a different language a foreign language which sounded like Russian but it wasn't Russian nor did she understand what the men in the hole replied the man rummaged in a chest and produced a rope to the rope he tied a mud-caked bucket and he lowered it carefully into the hole after a while he pulled it back up full of miry earth that smelled nasty he emptied it and once more he lowered it into the gaping hole the sun was sprawling in the sky and it was as if it were wheeling right above the street above the hole Beatrice could feel it on the top of her head

motionless she gazed vacantly at the broad glistening back of the digger

there was nobody passing on the street

In Bulgaria, nationalism is like a sailing ship, old but still afloat, driven by the wind of the people's discontent. Any pretext is good enough. For example, they celebrated liberation from the 'Ottoman yoke,' which took place one and a half centuries ago. Tens of thousands of people, most of them followers of the ultranationalist ATAKA movement, poured onto the streets, waving the Bulgarian flag and shouting slogans against the Turkish minority.

'I can't survive on a pension of fifty Euros,' complained one demonstrator, an old woman from the Black Sea tourist resort of Nessebar. 'People from Sofia have bought all the houses in the town, like the ex-minister of finance, Milan Velchev . . .

Everybody in Bulgaria should be forced to have a Bulgarian name, like what happens in the United States.'

Did I excerpt the above lines from a newspaper? I can't remember. They were written in a notebook, on whose cover is written in red capitals: THE BULGARIAN TRUCK. I think I found them on a website about the Balkans. I doubt they will be of any use to me.

his wife's name was Nina she was very young and she didn't want children it's too early she would say but he used to insist as a matter of fact not even he knew why he had got it into his head but she was having none of it not for the life of her I don't know how she managed it but she had got hold of some pills which she hid in a shoe in the bottom of the wardrobe so that Tsvetan wouldn't be able to find them she liked making love with him but she couldn't stand his long absences

I know what you get up to on the road how you go a-whoring left and right everybody knows that a truck driver finds himself a whore in every town he passes on the way

you're exaggerating he would half-heartedly say in his own defence

and I know it was precisely because she enjoyed being with him in bed that she missed him and it was hard for her to wait for him and so it's no wonder that one fine day she found herself a big strapping man in Sofia where she'd gone to buy herself a new dress Tsvetan had given her the money they no longer lived in Sofia but in a small town near the border with Macedonia she found herself a man from her mother's hometown of Zimnicea a Romanian who claimed he knew a cousin of hers and then they fell to talking and she realised that he wasn't making it up she didn't speak Romanian as well as she used to because she had been living in Bulgaria for a long time since when she was at primary school when her mother had fled from Romania she ran off with a Bulgarian some time in the 1980s after the death of Ceausescu she had gone back and forth across the Danube but she still knew a bit of the language

in any case Vașile could get by in Bulgarian they could each understand what the other was saying quite well and they booked into a hotel

I have stopped writing because I thought I heard the telephone ringing. I'm terrified ... At this hour it can't be Marianne. It's definitely not her, but maybe it is ... maybe it is the other woman, the other important female character who is going to take up more and more space in the book I'm writing. I haven't yet decided what name I'm going to give her.

In fact it wasn't the telephone. It was somebody ringing the doorbell. I open the door. A tearful teenage girl: Beatrice.

Victor is dying ... I didn't say anything. I stroked the top of her head. She pressed herself against me. And I didn't know what to do. What to say ... Her mother left them both a few months ago. Out of the blue. She didn't even leave a note. She just left. I don't know what got into me, what I mean is that I didn't even bother to mention this—what shall I call it? This departure, this abandonment of the conjugal home, although I'm not sure they were married or even partners (like most people are nowadays): she was a free woman, obsessed with being independent. She had gone off a couple of times before, even after the little girl was born, but Victor was in good health then, he could look after her. He raised her ...

It's my fault and I'm not even sure I needed a complication like this ... I ought to have been paying more attention. But now I've got no choice, I have to go on, taking into account this detail.

Detail?

I didn't know what to say. I held her close, I could feel her small breasts at the level of my belly, her little head reached just to my chin. Making an effort, I decided to disentangle myself from her, I pushed her away, but as her hands were clutching my trouser belt and pulling desperately, I was forced to make a show of being stern.

—What are you doing? Why are you pulling on my belt?

I would have made light of it, but Beatrice was now sobbing. I felt sorry for her. I thought that maybe she had an aunt or some relative who might take care of her. I don't even know her exact age.

Marianne can be right sometimes: I'm careless, I don't keep records, I treat my characters with a nonchalance akin to unfeelingness, and here I am, at a time like this, disconcerted, in other words I don't know how to get myself out of the mess I've created. And so I took her in my arms once more and hugged her tightly to my chest.

—Do you believe in God?

She was still snivelling. Maybe she didn't hear and so I repeated the question. She stopped crying, lifted her head and looked at me with puzzlement mingled with what might have been fear. She wasn't expecting such a question and nor did I know why I had put it like that, bluntly, indelicately. I probably wanted to draw her attention to the fact that at a time like that she needed to lean on something that transcended her and obviously I was also thinking about what was going to happen to her, now that she was all alone in the world. Utterly frightened, she looked at me and merely shook her head a few times, almost imperceptibly. She didn't believe . . .

She's doomed, I said to myself. Not for her mind Kantian morality, although, who knows, maybe Victor was wise enough to educate her in that direction, and his bitterness at having been abandoned by the girl's mother didn't plunge him into cynicism. Or illness.

Agreed, I have to find a subject.

Ultimately, it's not even all that complicated. At a pinch, I could even borrow one; I could filch one from another novel. I could pick one from a literary dictionary, for example *Le nouveau dictionnaire des œuvres*, published by Bompiani in partnership with Robert Laffont. True, it's a bit old, it lists only a very few contemporary novels, or rather almost none. So what! There are shitloads of subjects there, but it means my having to read at least a part of the synopses given in the three crabbed volumes of minuscule type—and that requires time and it is even more boring than reading one or more novels . . .

Perhaps it would be best to draw my subject from a film. There are lots of films. True, some of the scripts were inspired by novels. For example, I remember that Polish film, in fact no, I think it was Czech or maybe Hungarian, I can't remember, but the nationality of the actors and the director isn't important, we're living in the age of globalisation after all, I remember very well that the plot involved a truck filled with explosives—dynamite or even nitro-glycerine—and two drivers were taking turns behind the wheel. From time to time they'd bicker between themselves or recount all kinds of adventures, mostly in South America. They told their stories, and the viewer could watch them telling the stories, you didn't need to picture them in your mind like you do when you read. It was an exciting film. But I don't need two drivers; one is enough. A Bulgarian truck driver transporting crates of dynamite. Dynamite? Does he have any excuse for transporting dynamite on Europe's highways? Does he have a permit?

Now I realise that Marianne was right: it's important to know what's inside the crates stacked up in the back under the tarpaulin. In any event, the customs guards will find out. But are there customs guards anymore, now the borders have been opened thanks to the Schengen Agreement or whatever it's called?

The truck was being followed, not by customs guards, but by some hooligans looking for fun. They were playing a dangerous game: if they hit the truck too hard, the truck filled with nitro-glycerine, a substance that explodes in the blink of an eye ... I can't remember how the film ended, and I don't remember much about the other film, based on the novel by the important writer Marguerite Duras. To be honest, I haven't even seen it. I've just read about it. A woman is waiting for a truck ... Then what? I think there was also a man with her, an actor ... My memory is becoming obtunded, it's fraying with each passing day, and it's pointless to play the postmodernist, that is, to rewrite what has already been written, to revisit my predecessors, because my heart isn't in it. To do that I'd have to be younger, to have an intact memory, and to have read a whole heap of novels, and I haven't read very many, and the few I have read are jumbled up in the depths of my memory, which is gradually shrinking, like shagreen leather ... I found that one in a dictionary, I only knew the French expression, *peau de chagrin*—yes, of course, the Balzac novel, I haven't forgotten absolutely everything.

But in Balzac's day there weren't any trucks ...

Perhaps it's easier, in my case, I mean, to try to be original. Not to want to resemble other writers, even if you respect them and read them with pleasure. If you get around to reading them, that is. Worse is if you resemble them without reading them . . .

An original old man!

I'm talking about myself, obviously . . .

It's raining outside. A dense drizzle. I'm waiting for a phone call from—let's call her Milena—who wants at all costs for us to go dancing. Yes, that's right, to go dancing. She's discovered a dancehall, it's called *Georges et Rosie* and frequented mainly by older people like her or even older than her, as old as me. Milena laughs and slaps my thigh with her small, chubby hand:

—That's not true, she says, you look after yourself, you're in good shape.

I'm not crazy enough to contradict her. True, I still know how to handle women . . . But what about literature? In the last few years, I've only written literary reviews, most of them bilious and malicious. I even had a column, which I kept moving from one magazine to another: *Les frappes chirurgicales*. My publisher doesn't want to collect them in a single volume; he says he doesn't want to turn the whole of literary Paris against him. He's probably right.

Write a novel, he says, and I'll publish it right away.

In an antique shop I find an ivory statuette of Isis, or rather a bust.

—Don't you have an Osiris too? I asked

The owner took my arm and led me to the obscurest corner of the shop. Before speaking, he looked nervously left and right. I don't know whom he was afraid of, because the only other person in the shop was an elderly lady, who was bent double in front of some blue and green plates.

—I see you know your Egyptian antiques.

—Let's not exaggerate, I said modestly and at the same time eager for the truth. That bust was made in the nineteenth century, at the earliest. Many years after Napoleon's expedition to Egypt. If we had a magnifying glass, we could even find the date.

And I showed him the Isis, which I held cupped in the palm of my hand.

—Yes, of course. You're right. Anyway, the price is low . . . But you asked me about Osiris. Isis and Osiris . . . Like Tristan and Isolde, Abélard and Héloise, and so on.

—Ah, yes, right . . .

—Well, I had an Osiris, with a pointy beard and a helmet . . .

—A helmet?

—Whatever. I don't know what you call it.

—Nor do I.

—With the green or blue face of a drowned man . . . He was sitting next to Isis, as is only natural, I would look at them every now and again, and, please believe me, but I don't feel like parting with them. That's why I put them on the shelf at the back, as far back as possible, I stowed them away out of the sight of customers, collectors of Egyptian antiques . . .

—But Isis was in the window. That's where I saw her. If she had been in the back of the shop, I probably wouldn't have noticed her.

—Let me explain. Are you in a hurry?

—No, I'm not.

—Well, I was happy that nobody saw them where I'd put them. Very seldom, an elderly woman would creep up to them, like you did, and then my heart would shrink to the size of a flea. Sometimes, she'd ask the price. I would mumble something about the price not having been decided yet, which meant I couldn't tell her, I was waiting for an expert opinion, you know, it was only yesterday that I received the items from a Turkish friend who used to be ambassador to Egypt and who now lives in Paris, not far from the Eiffel Tower . . . So, I have them only for safekeeping. Well, I'm patient, the lady collector would say. I'll be back in a few days. I'm afraid the price will be rather high, I'd add.

More often than not, she didn't come back . . . There was only one who came back. And I played for time again. And she came back again. She gave a knowing smile. That is, I don't exactly know what was going on in her mind. In the end, I told her that the statuettes had already found a buyer and I had forgotten to pack them in the cardboard box: sold. The buyer was an Egyptian, sent all the way from the museum in Cairo. The old lady started to laugh. But she had no choice. She left.

The antique dealer was short and bald. He had blue eyes and a pale, almost yellowish face. He looked me up and down. He said no more.

—All right, I muttered, I take it you don't want to sell me the Isis . . . It's no big deal.

—Wait, I haven't finished, he said and grabbed me by the sleeve. I do want to sell it. You understand? Now that she doesn't have Osiris any more . . . I'm no longer as interested as I was before.

—But where is Osiris?

—I don't know, sighed the antique dealer. One fine day he vanished. The evening before they were both in the corner, where nobody could see them except for me. I had covered them with a yellow cloth. Nobody lifted the cloth. Only me . . . But the next day, when I opened the shop and slowly lifted the cloth, there was no one but poor Isis, lying on her belly, in despair: Osiris had vanished. I looked all around, on the shelf, underneath, but all I found was a cap, that elongated helmet or turban or whatever it's called. That was all that was left of him.

—Maybe a cat . . .

—I carefully swept the floor, but all I found were two fragments of body, a leg and an arm. Not an arm, a hand. There was probably a struggle; he must have put up a struggle against the person who wanted to kidnap him. I stopped looking. Where was I supposed to look? In any event, there was nothing else I could do. I couldn't rebuild him. Too much of him was missing.

I didn't know what to say. I searched for some consoling words, but couldn't find any. It was as if Isis had grown smaller in my palm. Yes, yes, she was shrinking visibly. Contracting. She had shrunk to the size of a USB stick. I didn't feel like buying her anymore. What was I supposed to do with her? I took the hand of the antique dealer, who was still staring into space, I turned it upwards, and I placed Isis in his palm.

after Victor's death she lived for a time with a kind of aunt who was called Nénette she was still at lycée I don't know which form she was in but what was for sure was that she didn't feel much like studying any more what is the point of wasting time learning all kinds of things that won't be of any use to you later on the aunt didn't much care about her niece's education it would even have suited her if Beatrice dropped out of lycée Nénette worked at a post office for quite a low wage and it would not be long before she retired why should she pay to keep her in lycée the next thing she knew she would be wanting to go to university to become an intellectual

why don't you learn a trade

what trade

hairdressing for example you're quite pretty you start out sweeping the floor

doing what

sweeping up it's no big deal until you learn the trade

isn't there a school

a hairdressing school

yes a school

I've no idea I'll try to find out I'll ask around

and so she ended up doing a hairdressing course but she didn't stick at it very long upon my word I really don't know what to do with her which direction to steer her in

I ought to have asked him what language to write it in. The novel . . . I've started to forget French now that I no longer write literature in French, which is changing, transforming itself with every new generation, like a moulting snake. And if I write it in Romanian, who will translate it? Given that in Romania they'll hardly be rushing out to read the book. Or in any other country, for that matter, in France, for example . . . How many readers have I had in France, my adopted homeland? I can count them on my fingers. Or maybe the translations have been to blame. Something very unpleasant happened to me after I started living in Paris: I realised that the more French I absorb, the less good the translations of my books seemed to be. In time I had become more exacting. Or rather, more demanding. Even though I was aware that for a translator it is not easy to adapt his style to that of the author, especially when the author is constantly trying to innovate. All right, I'm exaggerating . . . I'm boasting! The translator is a friend of mine. And my publisher is a wonderful man, he cares about his authors, he looks after them like a mother, there are very few who leave him; even though a time comes when you leave your mother, doesn't it? In any event, he's not to blame if I'm dissatisfied with a translation. The only solution is to translate my own books. After all, there was a time when I also wrote in French. That's probably what I'm going to do, especially given that poor Alain is ill, seriously ill, I don't even want to think about it . . .

Everybody says that an author cannot translate his own books, and nor is it a good thing if he does. He's capable of moving so far away from the original that he ends up writing another novel. But so what?

—And it might end up being worse than the original, jokes Paul, my publisher. I'm not even sure he is joking . . . I don't know why I am complaining. The thing is I'm not the only one. That's what writers do for you; they like to complain. Milena's publisher is much more important than mine and she still isn't satisfied. It's a publishing plant. The biggest literature factory in France is Gallimard . . . She's not satisfied, although she's certainly flattered that so important a publisher has faith in her. The thing is, she would like to have more readers. For that, the publisher would have to promote her books more. She sighs. At any rate to publish them in paperback. At least one. I'd like that too . . . That's wishful thinking, I told her. She married a Frenchman and she has striven to learn French. She's the same as me: a Francophone writer. Her mother tongue, that is, the language she is incapable of forgetting and of which she cannot rid herself, no matter how hard she tries, is Slovak. I've never dared to ask her what the difference is between Slovak and Czech. Nor why she got a divorce. Did she get married just so that she could get French citizenship? She could have learned French even if she had remained single.

Milena has blonde hair, but her skin is darker than mine. She smells nice, of quince.

it was not Nina that Tsvetan was thinking of now but his father whom he remembered as having been away all the time although his father wasn't a truck driver Tsvetan didn't even know what exactly it was he did he had heard all kinds of stories some used to say he worked for the secret police not for the Bulgarian secret police which didn't really count but for none other than the KGB he often used to visit Germany where he had a friend or rather a boss who bore an uncanny resemblance to Putin anyway after he died Tsvetan had found among his papers and other assorted documents a photograph tucked inside one of his numerous passports which were all in different names and in that photograph he was with Putin himself or else the person in the photograph looked terribly like him they were smiling at each other he didn't show it to anybody of course he had worshipped his father despite having seen him only a few times in his life the truth is that his father had more or less abandoned him and if Tsvetan had gone to high school it was thanks to an aunt who lived in Sofia she didn't have any children of her own and she had grown fond of him he didn't even know whether she was Kiril's sister that's what his father was called or whether she was her cousin or maybe the cousin of Rumiana who had died giving birth to him what is for sure is that when she found out that Kiril was dead Sonia was very upset she burst into tears and rolled off the bed on which she had lain down to answer the telephone she fell onto the carpet still holding the phone crying her eyes out

some people even went as far as to say that Kiril had been mixed up in the plot to assassinate the Pope not to condemn him but perhaps quite the opposite the truth is that the head of the Catholic Church was not much liked in Bulgaria where all the people were Orthodox Christians except for the Turks

but that was going too far the man who fired the pistol was a Turk called Mehmet Ali-Agca and it wasn't proven that he had accomplices and it would even seem that the CIA manipulated him so that he would cast the blame on the Eastern Bloc countries and on the KGB I've no idea

opinions were divided Tsvetan had even read a book about the conspiracy

Beatrice was standing motionless and looking at the broad

back of the digger it was hot the girl seemed fascinated with the rivulets of sweat that welled at the nape and trickled down around the shoulder blades as far as the small of his back where they merged at the spine and continued to descend until they reached the waistband of the blue duck trousers the digger at the edge of the hole or the ditch because the hole was getting longer it now looked like a trough bigger and bigger he looked at Beatrice again this time he gave her a more interested a more lingering look a more emphatic look Beatrice took two or three steps then stopped once more the digger had turned his back again and leaning over the hole he was looking at the diggers inside whom Beatrice couldn't see it meant that the hole or rather ditch was deep and no joke she took another step the digger said something in an unintelligible language he wasn't speaking French I don't know what language he was speaking how am I supposed to know but we might say that it was Bulgarian

from somewhere in the bowels of the earth there now came strange grinding noises albeit muffled the shovels no longer struck at the soil but something else that was neither wood nor metal it was as if it was hard scaly skin

a cry erupted it was a cry not of pain but of amazement
or of triumph

Yes, the man was none other than Depardieu. Not long before he became corpulent. But still massive. Sitting in front of him, at a table in that rather shabby, inner-city café, Marguerite was reading a script to him, written in the conditional mood. Yes, really! It would be too complicated to explain why . . . And nobody would be interested anyway. What is certain is that Depardieu, enraptured at what he was hearing, was gazing intently, his eyes were boggling from so great concentration, he looked simply hypnotised, which, let it go no further than ourselves, is hardly credible: in my opinion, the actor's mind was elsewhere, although his eyes were riveted on the plump woman in front of him, he was thinking of something else entirely, probably what kind of wine he was going to drink after he finished shooting the scene. It wasn't the film for him! That was for sure . . . In any event, it may be said that it relied on quite a strange screenplay, since it was being presented as a film proposal. But a film all the same. For, even if we can't see it, there was a camera somewhere nearby—filming! To me, this is something genuinely interesting: to describe a proposal, to comment on it, but discontinuously, giving just a few images from without, as it were. Sequences in which you see the truck rolling down the highway and the man at the wheel with a stony face that hints at nothing, not even tiredness. Beside him there is a woman. But no, I'm getting mixed up, I'm confusing it with a different film, it's not a woman, it's a man, the second driver. The woman will be hitchhiking. For the time being it looks like she is waiting in a café, with a glass or a cup of coffee in front of her, or a cup of tea, it doesn't matter what, she is waiting. Outside the wind is blowing. The woman is waiting; all she does is wait. She looks sad. And the truck driver has an inscrutable mien. He must be tired. He has come a long way. The truck is enormous. It's covered with a dark green tarpaulin, like a military truck. I like that. Why not tell Marianne that I like it? Call her on the telephone? No sooner said than done:

—Finally, I like it . . .

—Like what?

--*The Truck* by Margueritte Duras . . .

The line suddenly goes dead. I can't understand what's happening. I sit there holding the receiver, dumbfounded. About five minutes later, I telephone her again, but either she isn't there or she isn't answering, she suspects it's me again and she doesn't want to answer. It's obvious. She's upset. Or rather she's annoyed. So then—what else can I do? I start writing her another letter:

Marianne, I don't understand why you're so angry . . . You hung up the telephone on me. That's just the way you are. It doesn't take much to make you fly off the handle. But this time you didn't have a single reason to. Not one! What is so bad about my not liking Marguerite Duras, your favourite writer . . . Or maybe you thought I was being ironic, that I was making fun of you. I didn't have the right tone of voice. I'm sorry . . . I'm a bad actor. I admit it. It's true that the telephone isn't the most appropriate tool for maintain-

ing peace and harmony between people. You hear the voice, but you can't see the other person's face, his eyes. The information is incomplete. You can imagine anything at all about the other person. You're tempted not to let him speak, not to let him finish explaining himself. And then I . . . You know very well that I'm no good on the telephone. I'm utterly hopeless. I admit it. I can't speak, I can't find the most suitable tone of voice or words, I become aware of it, I get annoyed with myself, I tend to become monosyllabic, I can hardly wait for the conversation to end. No matter how hard I try, in the end I get grouchy, even impolite. That's why I prefer to write to you. Of course, when you call me on the telephone, I'm overjoyed to hear your voice, but I would also like to see your face. Please understand . . . The fact that I can't see you inhibits me. I'm sorry, but I can't get used to that particular tool of communication. I'm a writer, not an orator . . .

I delete the last sentence, which is unbelievably stupid.

But don't think that I'm writing to you just so I can complain about you hanging up on me. These things happen . . . It's not pleasant, obviously, but what can you do . . . I'm writing to ask you to help me find a subject. You're right: when you start writing a novel, you have to have thought of a story already, even if you alter it after that, even if you tidy it up here and there. And so I decided that the easiest thing to do would be to use a story that already exists, one that has been told before, at great length, by a heavyweight novelist, one of those ones from the nineteenth century, the century of the novel, the century of narrative. Balzac wrote a whole load of stories, but either I've forgotten them, or I never read them in the first place. Madame Bovary *I do remember. I know: it's not by Balzac. But even so . . . Madame Bovary is Flaubert or vice versa: Flaubert is Madame Bovary. I don't know who Balzac would be . . . What I mean is that I don't know which character he could be identified with so closely that you would be able to say Balzac is he . . . In any case, not Père Goriot, but sooner Eugène de Rastignac.*

Anyway, I digress. I should stop. But I think you get my point.

It won't come as any surprise to you if I tell you that I've never liked reading novels. I've written a few, because I wasn't capable of doing anything else. You will say that what I have written up to now aren't even novels, not even my most recent ones, where I strove to get as close to the reader as I could, to be not only readable, but to the reader's taste . . . The word is that I didn't really manage to pull it off. Both of you are right: you and the reader. You are also a character in it, and this is what annoyed you the most. I understand. 'I'm not jealous,' you said. 'I don't care what people say.' Well, I don't know whether things are really like that. What annoyed you the most (and with good reason!) is that I exaggerated when I narrated my extra-marital affairs: some of them I quite simply made up. Believe me . . . You're a bit of a braggart, you told me once. I don't know whether you were trying to disguise your annoyance by means of irony or vice versa. (What do you mean, vice versa?) I narrated, or rather invented, those affairs because that is what the public demands. The public is our master. People want love stories, sex scenes. That's what they want . . . Le grand public!

I acknowledge that I shouldn't have written it in the first person. But I let myself be influenced by those women novelists who are so fashionable nowadays. I took Christine Angot as my model. Why do you laugh? Don't you believe me? I don't have her talent, obviously. Nor have I experienced as much as she has: all those affairs, each more sordid than the next and narrated with such passion. Maybe she really did experience everything she narrates, especially in her latest novel, you know, the one about the singer who likes to fuck her from behind, taking pleasure in getting the two holes mixed up. Forgive me. I know you don't like crude language and that you believe it to be out of keeping with my advanced age. When you were young, you were more tolerant. Because back then I was capable of doing more than talk about it, whereas now . . . True, nowadays I would need something like a poetic context to be able to get down to, I mean, to get from the one thing to the other. Poetry is like a balm . . . All right, I'll erase that right now.

One day you told me, perhaps also in writing, that it was about time that I gave up this occupation, which suits me less and less the older I get. Meaning literature. Quite simply, I shouldn't write any more. Or, if I'm incapable of abandoning this rather outmoded pastime, I should content myself with writing articles for newspapers and magazines, here or in Romania. Am I dead set on fiction? Then the only thing is to write short stories like I did in my youth. With a short story I run less of a risk than I do with a novel. I'm in no danger of forgetting various aspects of my characters or, even worse, what they have already said. I have given serious thought to the things you said. I know . . . They weren't idle words. Nevertheless, I haven't been able to follow your advice. But anyway, given that I haven't got much time left, it no longer matters whether or not I write. It's of no importance whatsoever.

Recently I befriended a Slovakian writer named Milan. Or maybe it's Milen. I don't know. Milen or Milan, I'll ask him again. No, it's not Kundera. Kundera wouldn't give me a second glance: he's too famous. I sometimes see him on the street: he walks with a measured step, gazing into the distance, at the horizon. It won't be long before he is inducted into the Academy. The Académie Française, obviously. Didn't Bianciotti and Fernandez get in? You don't know who Bianciotti is? It's not important; you're not missing out on much. At least you know who Fernandez is! All kinds of other people have got into that Academy.

I met Milen at the Book Fair. He's Slovakian, but he has been writing in French for a few years. Like me . . . Granted, it's quite seldom that I write in the language: newspaper articles, literary reviews or whatever you want to call them, but I did write in it years ago. In any event, that's what I said to him: that I'm a Francophone writer too, like him. He laughed. 'What does "Francophone writer" mean?' he asked. Well, it's a writer who speaks French and even writes in French. 'Why not a French writer?' I didn't know what to say to that. I tried to wriggle out of it. I started mumbling. You get it: he thinks of himself as a French writer and reckons that Francophone writer is an antechamber category. 'What kind of category?' I asked. And I laughed, because in fact I understood very well what he was getting at. When you become famous, you also automatically become French. Automatically . . .

Of course, the French are very nationalistic. I'm not sure whether that's the most suitable term . . . Let's say they're self-obsessed. They're very exacting with others, with those who want to write in French, although French is not their mother tongue. They didn't imbibe it with their mothers' milk, as somebody or other once said.

But isn't that normal? All those centuries of French literature! And what a literature! What great writers they have had! And still have, even today . . . Think of Beigbeder or an authoress like Camille Laurens.

Milen gave a hearty laugh, tossing his head back. He's younger than me. How much younger? I don't know . . . I can't tell and I'm embarrassed to ask. He's blond and quite plump. Not very tall, in fact you might even say he's short. It doesn't matter. He looks good. But his skin is quite dark. I don't know why. Maybe he uses a sunbed. In the end, why not? There's nothing to be ashamed of. Sunbeds aren't just for women . . .

But I'm starting to ramble and I wouldn't want to annoy you. If we had been talking on the telephone, you would have hung up on me long before now. But this way you are forced, if only from pure curiosity, to read to the end. Even if what I write annoys you, you control yourself. What else could you do? Tear up the letter? Crumple it up and toss it in the wastepaper basket . . . Don't do that, because you would need an audience. Otherwise, why do it, if nobody can see you? It's the same with the telephone: when you hang up on me, I am the audience, the receptor for your annoyance. But with a letter you are on your own. But don't worry: I won't ramble for much longer. I also have other things to do. One of them is to continue with my novel. In any event, you will have understood what it is I want, what I am getting at: I want you to help me find a subject. It's no big deal for you. You've read masses of novels, mostly Anglophone ones, novels where all kinds of exciting things happen. And your memory is capacious and accurate. Not like mine. Mine is like a dog's dinner.

have a pleasant journey and come back in good health said the old woman in her solemn croaking voice

Tsvetan looked down at her from the cab of the truck as she walked away slightly stooped

all the best and he started the engine

after driving for about fifty kilometres or more he looked to his right and saw the umbrella leaning against the back of the seat upholstered if not in genuine leather then with a similar-looking plastic material the umbrella was the same colour as the back of the seat and that was probably why he didn't notice it sooner how the hell did she manage to leave it there she was probably in a hurry when she climbed down out of the cab and forgot it it's hardly a reward and she didn't leave it on purpose

in annoyance Tsvetan bangs the steering wheel with the palm of his hand

what is he supposed to do now he can hardly turn back for the sake of a wretched umbrella apart from anything else it's dangerous even if he's not on the motorway and the next village where he could turn around without any danger is still far away the old woman probably needs the umbrella that's why she brought it with her but even so it's hard to believe that she is still there at the spot where she got out of the truck waiting

it's her loss

if he thinks about it more the old woman even seemed a little suspect because of her headscarf her face wasn't really visible only her nose which was quite hooked and her eyes were quite cunning although he only looked her in the face once and she had the large long-boned body of a man maybe it wasn't even a woman Tsvetan smiled and pressed the accelerator he overtook a semi-trailer truck then another smaller truck covered with a green tarpaulin although it wasn't a military truck at the back there was quite a large space that had been left uncovered inside he thought he could see coffins neatly stacked up one on top of the other yes he was almost certain the truck was laden with coffins after he overtook it and pulled back into the right-hand lane and then in front there appeared a column of automobiles one after the other maybe an official motorcade although ordinary-looking the car in front blazing the trail was probably a police car

he looked at the umbrella again

how could it have been a man she had a long black skirt and on top a plum-coloured anorak and a headscarf also black he couldn't remember how she was shod he hadn't seen her shoes but they might have been boots

he smiled again

the truck with the coffins had caught up with him and was overtaking him driven by a man with a bushy walrus moustache the coffin driver was laughing he was sticking his thumb up at him he was laughing his head off Tsvetan accelerated too a proper race was underway lasting for kilometres and kilometres it was really dangerous

Slovenka/A Call Girl, 90 min., director: Damjan Kozole (Slovenia—Germany—Serbia—Croatia—Bosnia Herzegovina)

Alexandra (23) is studying English in Ljubljana. Nobody knows that Alexandra takes out small ads using the pseudonym 'Slovenian girl' and that in fact she makes her living from prostitution. Highly skilled at manipulating men, she is a consummate liar, with a slight tendency to kleptomania. The only person she really cares about is her father, a washed-up rocker. Alexandra has plans for the future, but her life proves to be more difficult than she expected.

—In your other novels it was as if you were in search of characters. You wandered here and there, from country to country, you roamed the length and breadth of Europe under that pretext. You agonised over finding characters. The author and his characters . . .

Marianne pauses. The thing is that she's wrong. Yet further proof of how superficially she reads my books: the author wasn't looking for them, but the other way around, Marianne! The characters were in search of the author . . . It's not the same thing!

But I don't dare to contradict her. I let her go on nagging me. It does her good to let off steam once in a while. Maybe afterwards she'll be more understanding. Gentler.

—Now you're in search of a subject . . .

—Well, yes . . .

—You're not even capable of coming up with a subject.

There are a few moments of silence at both ends of the line. Does it really run along the seabed? The line . . . The telephone line! I hear that nowadays we communicate by satellite. So there isn't a line anymore? Anything scientific or technical quite simply bewilders me. It's not just that I don't understand any of it, but it makes me dizzy even thinking about it. I'm not exaggerating, not even one little bit. Or only very slightly . . .

Marianne has sweetened her tone. Now she is whispering to me tenderly, as if we were both lying down next to each other and moving our heads, lips and ears closer to each other on the same pillow:

—Describe a dream . . .

—A dream?

—A dream. Or two dreams, combining them both. What do I know? You're the writer. Or at least so you claim. A writer . . .

—All right, but I don't dream.

The tenderness evaporates, the whisper turns to a hiss:

—How can you not dream! Everybody dreams. If you don't dream, it means you're abnormal. How then can you have the gall to address normal readers? Readers that dream . . .

—Readers that dream! I repeat in a whisper, as if I were afraid lest somebody hear me.

I look all around me. I'm alone. Through the window all that can be seen is the wall of the next building, a blank wall, without windows, a grey blind wall. Above it, a strip of sky that can't quite manage to turn blue.

She's probably making fun of me. I wouldn't put it past her . . .

—Offer the reading public something different than what they see out of the window every day. That's what I mean.

—Yes, well . . .

—And stop complaining that nobody buys your books . . .

I couldn't stand it anymore. I hung up.

in a box Victor had kept photographs of her when she was little look in this photograph she can't have been two years old yet a tousled mop of dark hair beneath which the large dark eyes filled the whole of the little face in this one she's walking waddling like a duck yes it's obvious that she's waddling tottering with her arms outstretched trying to find her balance

here she is sitting on the bed and looking straight into the camera without a trace of a smile either in her eyes or on her lips

in another she is in the grass not far from the stream Victor photographed her from behind while she was looking for snails or for hedgehogs she was a little older here she was squatting with her arm outstretched

tears welled in his eyes when he looked at them

After all, a monologue is different than a letter, and the art of the novel, in which monologues intertwine with dialogues, is the art of complexity . . . You can't say that such commonplaces don't have their own role to play: quoting them prolongs the text, dilutes it, makes it more readable. What's more, the reader is happy at being able to grasp the profundity of the author's idea, and he will even play his part in disseminating it. The next day, he will tell his wife or friend:

—You know, the art of the novel is the art of complications. Hold on, that's not it . . . It's the art . . .

—Of complications? wonders the friend, calmly sipping his mug of beer.

Then he wipes the foam from the corner of his mouth with a napkin. He dabs delicately and waits for the other to clarify his idea.

—No, that's not it. It's the art of complexity, I tell you. Of complexity . . . You understand what I mean?

—The art of complexity, of course . . .

It's the same with punctuation. Even if it's nice to write without punctuation, even if the absence of punctuation can be justified in the case of the monologue, it's wise that the writer not abuse it. He would do well to consider the reader. Meaning none other than Tsvetan, who apparently never got further than primary school. He also went to high school, you say? Very nice! But did he graduate? Did he sit his baccalaureate? And how many books has he read since then? And what kind of books? He read that book about the conspiracy . . . Very good! And what else has he read? True, with his job it's impossible. You can't expect him to read while he's driving. He listens to music, no problem there . . . Pop music, granted, but music nonetheless. Sounds making up a melody that is squeezed in the clamp of a rhythm that becomes obsessive. Most of the time the words are in English, which has been of great help to him in absorbing a language that is absolutely necessary in our day and age. An imperial language! The language of globalisation . . . He likes to call it the American language . . .

And when he stops for the night, preferably in a town, or a largish village, then as you can imagine, he abandons himself to entertainments more pleasant and more bracing than reading.

He likes women, and women like him. And what is there not to like: you've seen his biceps, pectorals and nape, his dark, oily eyes, his trousers moulded over his muscular legs, so skin-tight that his genital organ stands out strongly, with the result that it looks more protuberant than other men's. Perhaps it really is . . . Are women sensitive to such external signals? I don't know for sure. Probably. Why wouldn't they be? Although there is always a risk. You can be mistaken and end up with a pansy, a wimp. There's always a degree of risk. You have to weigh these external signals in relation to the overall behaviour of the male. If he doesn't waver, if he aims straight at the target, then it means he doesn't have any complexes, he's not afraid to abide by the ancient code, which has remained more or less unchanged in its essence. Although there can be no doubt that it is the woman who makes the choice, it is fit and proper that she pretend to be a little timorous, hesitant, and then the man will have to be insistent, even to act a little rough. But he has no choice: that's the game . . .

It wasn't like that with Milena. I didn't go right up to her. It was she who came to up me. To be more precise, it was as if she came *en marche arrière* . . .

I was at a cocktail party held in honour of some female writer or other who had just won the Femina Prize. It's only very rarely that I go to cocktail parties, and I was there completely by accident: I had bumped into a critic on the street, a journalist who also writes literary criticism, an ass-kisser, he possesses neither style nor backbone, he writes almost exclusively about the authors of two publishing houses, they probably slip an envelope stuffed with money in his pocket every now and again, I wouldn't swear by it, but that's what people say . . .

—Let's go to the cocktail party, said he.

—What cocktail party? I'm not in the mood . . .

—In honour of Mme What's-her-name. There'll be food, and above all lots to drink. Come on!

So I went. There were already a lot of people there. I also spotted a few writers published by Éditions P.O.L. Some of them pretended to recognise me. But they had difficulty pronouncing my name. The French have great problems with foreign names. They even mangle English and American names. In other words, they pronounce them à la française. It's a throwback from the days when the whole world spoke French. The intellectuals, I mean to say, the ones who travelled and met people from other countries. Why make the effort of learning a foreign language when they could make themselves understood in their mother tongue, which is to say, in French. Other people learned in their stead, the ones eager to communicate with them. True, this isn't the whole of the story. Also to blame is the accent. If it's so hard for them to speak a foreign language, it's not only because of their acute self-centredness, which nowadays seems downright ridiculous, like a top hat on man wearing an undershirt. An undershirt that is too short, exposing his belly button. Nowadays, when the whole world speaks English. I don't know whether that's a good comparison. It's a rather humorous one, albeit slightly exaggerated, I admit. In the end, it doesn't matter.

And so there I was, talking to a very nice P.O.L. author, about whom I had written a number of glowing articles—it didn't take much effort, as I genuinely like him—and he was telling me that he played chess and that we should play each other some time. I smiled benignly. Why not? As a rule, writers are cack-handed when it comes to playing chess. But as Igor is Russian, maybe he won't be such a walkover . . . I mumbled my consent and knocked back my glass of vodka. He knocked his back and moved away. He had nothing else to say to me. He could hardly have talked to me about my novels or lauded them when he hadn't even read them. At least he had read the articles I wrote about his novels. But how then did he know I'm a good chess player? Obviously, he must have read the back-cover blurbs. That's still something!

Left alone, there was nothing else for it except to go to the barman and have him refill my glass. There was still vodka left, but the champagne had just about run out. In front of me, holding out her glass, a woman with hair dyed Venetian blonde turned her head to me and looked at me with her blue, all-of-a-sudden quizzical eyes. She had prominent, Slavic cheekbones. She was between thirty and forty. I'm no good at gauging women's ages. In any case, she looked very young . . . In comparison with myself, I mean.

—There's no more champagne, she said.

—Not a problem. I don't like champagne. I'd rather drink a little vodka.

She took the glass from my hand and held it out to the barman. Vodka! And the same for herself. She leaned forward as she held out the glass, touching me with her bottom, which wasn't very large, but was shapely, firm, muscular. The shock triggered a small chemical reaction inside me, the blood immediately descended to the bodily part being touched and, as she was still in a leaning position, waiting for the barman to get round to filling the two glasses, she felt the transformation, she even encouraged it, bracing her buttocks against the particular spot, which was now gurgling with blood.

Afterwards, our conversation lasted not even five minutes. From her very first words I discovered that her publisher is Gallimard. She was delighted to hear that I am with P.O.L., a publishing house that has seen a meteoric rise since coming under the wing of her own. That's how she put it. Since being given a leg up, in other words. Nonetheless, that doesn't prevent it from remaining independent. To a certain extent . . . We both laughed. Then we polished off the vodka in our glasses and went out the door: she assured me that she lived nearby, on a neighbouring street, and that she had some genuine Russian vodka at home.

And she lifted her buttocks so high that, carried away, and without intending to, I planted myself somewhat lower: it doesn't matter, it's good there too, she whispered, and she had a slightly Slavic accent that was rather agreeable.

If you start speaking a language after the age of twelve or thirteen—I read this somewhere, in a work on linguistics or phonetics—then no matter how hard you try, you will never get rid of your native accent, or else you would have to have a perfect musical ear, although even then it would still be hard, because the vocal cords are already formed, the whole throat . . .

—Not now, not right away, go and wash.

And so I went.

Since she arrived in New York, Marianne has been getting lazier and lazier when it comes to writing. Not that she was ever a graphomaniac. She would say: I prefer reading. With me it's the opposite. In fact, I'm not so sure. With her I preferred making love. At least that's what I would tell her . . .

She's not to be outdone:

—And I do with you, too, says Marianne.

—Me too . . .

—With whom?

—With you, of course, but for that it's recommendable that we be as close to each other as possible, preferably in the same bed.

—Don't be pedantic!

She doesn't write, and so she picks up the telephone instead. Sometimes she even calls me in the middle of the night, her excuse being that she doesn't know how to work out the time difference. 'There's a difference of six hours,' I tell her, but without deluding myself, especially given that her answer is so disarming: 'Is that what you think?'

Last night, when I got back home, no sooner had I closed the front door than the telephone rang.

—Did I wake you up? she asked.

—I was reading . . .

—You were reading?

—Yes, why are you so amazed? It does happen on occasion. I couldn't sleep. And so I was reading . . .

—In that case I can't be disturbing you all that much.

—No, you're not, but I'd like to go and get a glass of water. I'm very thirsty.

—Reading makes you thirsty?

—Sometimes.

—And what do you drink when you're thirsty?

—What do you mean?

—Whiskey or vodka?

—This is why you're phoning me at two in the morning? To ask what I like to drink?

—Is it two in the morning?

—It is here . . .

—And there I was worrying myself that you might not be at home . . .

I'm not sure whether she is being ironic, rather gratuitously—because with her irony stands in for humour—or whether she is jealous, whether she suspects something, although not even she knows what exactly. This is the most interesting phase of jealousy, but also the trickiest for both parties: when you don't know why exactly you are jealous.

—Come on, we'd better go to bed. To sleep.

—I can't. I haven't had dinner yet.

—You're right there, you can't . . .

—I phoned you earlier. You weren't at home.

—That's entirely possible. I was at a cocktail party.

—I phoned you half an hour ago.

—I was probably on the toilet.

—Then you must be ill. You must have diarrhoea. You should take something.

—Why do you say that?

—Because I also phoned you an hour ago. Were you on the toilet then, too?

I remain silent for a few moments. I don't know what to say. I cough. I'm very thirsty. After the vodka and everything else. Finally, I decide to mount a counterattack.

—This is how you spend your time? Instead of eating, sleeping, resting. You need to lead a calm, orderly life now that you're undergoing medical treatment. You know very well! Your doctor told you so.

At the other end of the line there isn't a sound. I don't think she has hung up. I would have heard something, a click, a clack, a sound however faint. She has left the telephone off the hook, on the bedside table or the bed, or maybe on the kitchen table, and she has gone into another room. I know she is staying with a girlfriend, her name is Laura, in fact no, Laura doesn't live in New York anymore, I don't know where she lives now. I've lost track of her. Maybe she has gone back and is living in New York again. Anyway, it's not important.

Marianne left three months ago to take a course of medical treatment not available anywhere else. Everybody says that the Americans are still the best in the field of medicine. I didn't go with her when she started her treatment. I had a public reading in Brussels. Now I regret it. Why do I regret it? Because I need to be able to situate my interlocutor (I don't like saying that Marianne is a literary character) in a specific and familiar place. In any case, the reason I hate talking on the telephone is that I can't see the other person, and that annoys me. It's even worse when you can't even picture the place from where the other person is speaking. There are telephones that display an image of the person you're talking to. Or aren't there? Well, that's what they tell me. I'm going to suggest that she buy one, although I'm not sure it's such a good idea: she'll want me to buy one too. And then it will be hold on to your hats: the telephone will be ringing every hour of the night and day. I don't think it would be worth the trouble . . .

instead of going to the hairdressing college she roamed the streets and I don't know how but she mainly ended up on those streets where the diggers were toiling stripped to the waist with their broad sweaty backs Beatrice never grew tired of looking at them

one day one of the diggers who was leaning on his shovel and looking from time to time at the ones in the hole maybe he was giving them instructions or orders he was a kind of boss or foreman one day he turned his head towards her and waved for her to come closer

Beatrice might very well have not gone over or even run away she had enough time in any event the man wouldn't have run after her that street was deserted but there were passersby on the nearby streets she had even seen a policeman on a bicycle pedalling furiously

once again the digger waved at her to come over and she went with slow steps dragging her feet but she still went then the digger smiled a single brief smile more of a rictus but a smile of satisfaction he took her in his arms and lifted her up and Beatrice didn't struggle but when she reached the bottom of the hole a hole not as deep as the others a hole abandoned because it didn't point in the exact direction chosen by the diggers it was only then that she attempted to protest although she realised that she didn't stand the slightest chance of escaping from the brawny arms of the labourer who had tossed his shovel to one side he lifted up her dress and tore off her panties he quite simply ripped them off

she was writhing convulsively like a decapitated hen it hurt terribly and the man couldn't manage to penetrate her

stop moving around he muttered

but even if she stayed perfectly still and spread her thighs as wide as she could it still wasn't easy the digger was forced to thrust and pull back then to thrust vigorously until after repeated attempts he succeeded during which time her body was abused in every conceivable way

Beatrice was sobbing softly

One evening, Milena asked me whether I would like her to read to me her latest novel, which she was still working on. I had no choice. I couldn't refuse, even though I felt sleepy and I was afraid of falling asleep while she read. I said: 'Great idea!'

The narrator, who seemed to be one and the same person as the author (nowadays everybody writes or pretends to write autobiographical fiction, it's the trend!), is in a castle in Italy, not far from Florence, where she has been invited by a marquis who fancies himself as a patron of the arts and literature: a conceited, pretentious character. But also filthy rich. Of course, she's not the only guest. The marquis has got it into his head to lend a hand to the process of globalisation, but at the cultural level, obviously. And so there is also an Englishman there, by the name of James, and writers of other nationalities, including an

Indian, whose name I forget. I do remember, however, that unlike other Indian writers, he doesn't write in English, although he speaks the language perfectly, as the author assures us, or to be more precise, the narrator, who, like Milena, is Slovakian and writes in French. The Englishman, who is something of an eccentric, has a rat in his room, which he keeps in a spacious silver cage. A kind of pink rat. The Englishman's fear is that the cat he's seen walking across the lawn in front of the castle, a black tomcat as big as a dog, might one day bump off his protégé. In vain does the narrator assure James that the tomcat would have no way of entering his room uninvited, unlike her, whom he has invited to tea at a quarter past five.

—And you've absolutely nothing to fear from me, quipped Milena, or rather the narrator. I won't so much as look at him.

—At whom? asked the English writer, whose mind was probably on something else.

—At the rat.

However strange it might seem, he found her words downright insulting. It's rare for an Englishman to be completely devoid of any sense of humour. Or perhaps he didn't get Central European humour. There is a kind of rivalry between these two types of humour. What's for sure is that he was on the verge of showing the Slovakian woman the door. He barely controlled himself. For a good few minutes he uttered not one word. They were both silent. It was obvious that they had nothing more to say to each other. Milena got up and left. It was twenty-five past five; the tea in the teapot was undrunk. The Englishman made no move to stop her; he spoke not a word. He didn't even see her to the door. Milena left with her tail between her legs, if I may put it like that.

To tell the truth, it wasn't James she'd set her sights on, but on somebody else entirely: an Iraqi, who was a kind of factotum at the castle, since he did the shopping and fixed the antiquated, unreliable plumbing in the rooms, and especially the bathrooms. He occasionally slept with the cook. His name was Tariq.

One sunny Sunday, a superb day that brought out the best in the surrounding landscape, with its svelte cypresses like mediaeval knights on hills that were like frozen waves, the narrator climbed into Tariq's pickup truck and they both went for a picnic in the Tuscan countryside.

—It's splendid! I say enthusiastically.

— Do you really think so?

Milena was left literally open-mouthed. But I didn't look like I was being ironic, and indeed I wasn't, I assure you, but being a sincere admirer of the Tuscan landscape—I had been there the year before with Marianne, not far from Pienza—my mouth had simply run away with me.

—And did you sleep with Tariq? I asked in a whisper, realising that she hadn't liked my interruption.

She didn't answer right away. She lifted her head and looked out of the window, although there was nothing to see there apart from a few stars scattered between the clouds. It was almost midnight. And then she looked me in the eye and said, also in a whisper:

—Not me, the narrator . . .

he's bought himself a portable *ordinateur* a very small one a laptop in fact when he's driving he places it on the passenger seat and looks at it from the corner of his eye from time to time and his right hand quickly taps at the keyboard—the page is already open at Google—typing the word *truck* for example

I'm joking . . .

for a while she was a cashier in a shoe shop on the rue Saint Denis a few metres away on a side street there was a sex shop they were everywhere in that neighbourhood but it isn't clear why that particular side street sex shop attracted her more than the others one evening she went up to the shop also obviously lured by the illuminated sign it was a kind of cabaret offering striptease on the sign it said *Vertige d'amour* she didn't stop she went on her way she still lived at Nénette's the aunt who was waiting to retire Beatrice decided that it was time to rent a room for herself not far from the shop she spoke to a coworker from Martinique a very nice girl with whom she got on very well they could share a room if it was big enough they could put two beds in why two better one big one and they burst out laughing

one Sunday they went to view a room on the seventh floor in fact no it was on the sixth with no elevator on the same street as the cabaret that Beatrice liked she was determined to sign the lease on the room as quickly as possible and inform her aunt but the next day she quarrelled with her boss who out of the blue wanted to sleep with her but she didn't want to or rather she would have liked to but at first she refused he flung her without any preliminaries on the decrepit couch in the back room and he was already dropping his trousers and getting ready to whip out his schlong he was in a hurry but probably she didn't do what she was supposed to given she was lacking in experience she didn't even take off her panties just her skirt and after tugging on her blouse like a madman and trying to pull it over her head he abruptly went flaccid and it was pointless her finally ridding herself of her blouse and deciding that it was about time she took her panties off when she saw him pulling his trousers back up and she felt like laughing she sniggered behind her hand as you can imagine that could hardly make things better

he fired her

she didn't even tell her aunt

she went straight to the Vertige d'amour in the corner of the window there was a piece of yellowing card inscribed in capital letters WE'RE HIRING DANCERS

'Rien n'est vrai dans le réel,' said Marguerite Duras.

Yet another commonplace?

Milena is an intelligent, cultivated woman; you can converse with her about anything, especially when it comes to literature. This is why I sometimes even make a foray into literary theory with her, a subject area that most writers look down on. Or else, for some unknown reason, they pretend not to be interested in it: neither in the theory nor in the jargon that goes along with it, all those supposedly pretentious terms that to them don't say anything much. Talent should be left to gambol across the meadow like a foal. Free to neigh to its heart's content . . . Marianne falls into this category, although she is not a writer; but she is the wife of a writer and she worked at a publishing house for I don't know how many years, reading countless books, many more than I've read.

This is why I was pleasantly surprised to find out that Milena knew not only about Egyptian mythology, but also what is known in literary theory as the 'Osiriac device.' Once, when we were talking about it, the subject of characters came up.

—When it comes to characters, I said, we might very well apply the Osiriac device here.

—How so?

—Very simply. How do we go about creating a character? Whence do we take him? From the reality around us, where else? But note! It's not a good thing to transpose *tale quale* the qualities of a real person, which would result in a *roman à clef*, you see . . . Given we're playing with symbols, it's the same method that pushes us into allegory. As a rule, however, we construct a character by combining the features of a number of people. Let's call it the classic method.

—Classic it may be, but I can't think of any other method. Even in science fiction . . .

—All right, I would like to apply the Osiriac device here, which in Ricardou's theory applies to meaning, and sometimes also to the subject; that is, I conceal a single character under the guise of multiple characters. I cut Osiris into pieces and scatter him throughout the narrative. Isis, the well-versed reader, the sister and wife of Osiris, the one who seeks meaning in the diversity of the words, will strive to put him back together, to make him whole. The others will have their own reading. That's up to them . . . A text always has multiple readings. What is more, I'm of a mind to do it in such a way that Isis and Osiris will be one and the same person. Do you understand? Isis will be seeking herself . . .

—I understand that you're starting to ramble, snaps Milena and all of a sudden I hear the voice of Marianne. Except that her eyes aren't blue, but dark, like Laura's . . . In fact no, like Beatrice's, I mean . . .

Danet asked her whether she had done ballet at school and

she answered yes but not at school her parents enrolled her in a private dance course the girls there were between eight and fourteen years old she didn't like it much she dropped out after just a few months

grip the pole ordered Danet

Beatrice wrapped her hands around the pole and began to spin around holding on with both hands then with one hand flexing one leg gracefully and thrusting it behind her as far as she could Danet seemed satisfied although the number was not ready yet they still had to work on it for a good few days

now take off your bra

she stopped rotating and took off her bra it wasn't easy she was out of breath

she had breasts like yellow watermelons smaller and more oval than usual or rather they were like plump pears only slightly tapering later she saw a painting in the Louvre she entered by chance one Sunday afternoon a painting by Titian and indeed the resemblance was striking except that she was somewhat thinner than the woman painted by the Venetian artist different times different attitudes stay as you are the boss's admiration was sincere she had no doubt

now we have to set up the guillotine said Danet and two goons came in lugging and pushing a contraption that really did look like a guillotine the blade the boss assured her is made of cardboard you can touch it if you like it isn't dangerous

Danet kept eyeing her up but he waited a number of days before sleeping with her he didn't kiss her he didn't caress her take it in your mouth she took it quite a big one but rather soft and her sex was not very receptive most of the time it wouldn't enter at all probably what was needed were longer preliminaries than he had the patience for and than he was used to with the other girls it's amazing I've never seen the like before

Danet rested on his hands above her and didn't dare to touch her breasts with his mouth to suck them or even kiss them for some unknown reason that clumsiness or impatience on his part touched her she pulled him towards herself pressed his head to her breasts and then there was no longer any need for him to be inside he ejaculated immediately stickily splotching her pubic hair with sperm that spread to her belly button

now with both hands take off your panties that's right very nice arch your back come on a bit more

his voice strong at first would falter as Beatrice took off her bra then her panties in the morning at rehearsals and in the evening he would applaud enthusiastically along with the other customers or drinkers the music would stop and everybody would admire her well-proportioned body and they would all be enchanted astounded by her pelt of thick black hair that sprouted like a squirrel's tail from her fofoloancă

then the guillotine was pushed to the front and she would kneel with calculated slowness lay her neck on it in the textbook position with both her hands resting on the apparatus that looked terrifyingly like a real guillotine silence would descend all around they would all be holding their breath and she would also be the one who activated a barely visible mechanism and the blade would fall with a dull thud the spectators glasses in hand would shout like at a revolution greatly excited by the rivulets of blood that were trickling on to the floor and even welling into a small red puddle that would soon form a crust coagulate and dry

they knocked back their drinks and right away ordered another round to quench the burning thirst in their throats

The telephone was ringing. I heard it as if in a dream. I wasn't asleep, but nor can I say I was fully awake. The night before I had drunk too much, I had been to the Vertige d'amour, a nightclub and striptease joint; I don't know what got into me. In fact I do know . . . I was hoping to see Beatrice, but that night she wasn't there, I don't know why.

And so it was after midnight by the time I got back, quite flustered, and I barely managed to get to sleep. And now I was too tired to get up. I don't know why I don't put the telephone on the bedside table, so that I would just have to reach out my hand to pick up the receiver.

The telephone was still ringing, seemingly louder and louder. It wouldn't stop ringing. It had to be Marianne. And so I made an effort and dragged myself to the coffee table where I left it the day before after I spoke to Milena.

—Hello? Hello?

Obviously, it was Marianne, who, with unwonted politeness, apologised if she had woken me up.

—You were probably working until after midnight. On your novel.

—Um, yes . . .

—Very good! That's the spirit . . .

She has seen the English translation of a book of mine in a bookshop in central New York.

—You wrote it a long time ago, she says. You were young and full of energy. Back then you had a certain amount of talent . . .

—Better you tell me what it is you want to say. Why did you call me?

—I called you to try to persuade you . . . and I don't want you to take it the wrong way, because I care about you. About you, and about you the writer, do you understand?

—I understand, but I don't know what it is you want . . . Persuade me to do what?

—To try to persuade you, although I know how stubborn you are . . . To persuade you not to write without punctuation anymore, because it's not good . . . Do you understand? Not for anybody! Neither for readers nor for critics. Not to mention the translator . . .

—The translator?

—Yes, yes, I talked to your English translator.

—To Camiller?

—Yes . . . Wasn't he the one who translated *The Something-or-other Wedding*?

—Yes, he was. But he's also translated other books.

—How wonderful . . . I met him in a bookshop. He's a very nice man and not lacking in charm.

—What do you mean?

—I'm saying that he is a charming man. As strong as a bear and as calm as a tomcat . . . We went to a café, where we had a chat about your novels.

—I didn't know you knew Patrick . . .

—Don't say you're jealous of your own translator!

—I'm not jealous at all, but I didn't know . . .

—What didn't you know?

—I didn't know you knew him.

—Well, I didn't know him. He started talking to me. I was in a bookshop. He said: 'Aren't you Marianne?' 'Yes, that's my name.' 'I recognised you. You know, it was I who translated the book you're holding.' 'Pleased to meet you,' I said, 'but I'm not in the book . . . You've got the wrong one.'

—You are in *Hotel Europa*, I yell into the receiver. He translated that one too.

—Granted. That's what he told me as well. 'Maybe you are in other ones too,' he added.

—Well, he's right . . .

—Maybe he is, but what I'm saying is that I'm not in all your books. It is pointless Paul's complaining . . .

—Who?

—Paul, your French publisher. You have so many now that you get them mixed up!

—Paul is worried about the readers . . . Isn't it natural? A publisher wants to have as many readers as possible. That's what every publisher dreams of: readers pouncing like wild beasts on the books he publishes, snatching them from the shelves of bookshops, fighting each other for them, punching, kicking, and then one of them will manage to go to ground in some corner of the bookshop, clutching the book to his chest, whereupon he will literally devour it. It's the dream of every normal publisher. It's natural . . .

—Obviously. But you were the one who said that Paul isn't a normal publisher. And if he really does want to have as many readers as possible, then he's made a losing bet when it comes to you. I feel sorry for him . . .

There's nothing I can say to that. I wait for her to resume the conversation. Nothing is audible at the other end of the line. Is it really a line? I don't think so. It will have been in the past. It was probably laid along the seabed, under the nose of the sharks; I wonder how they refrained from severing it with their steely teeth.

At last I hear Marianne's voice once more. She is shouting

into the receiver, she is far away, over the ocean and she's probably afraid I can't hear her. Please, use commas, use full stops, dialogue hyphens and even semi-colons, the way you learned at school, not ellipses . . . the reader will appreciate it when, flicking through the book in the bookshop, he is wavering as to whether to buy it . . .

After we worked up a sweat dancing at *Georges et Rosie*—the tango, of course, as I don't really know any other dance—we went to a striptease joint. We sat down at a table as close as possible to the locus of defoliation . . . Milena liked my lexical invention and said that she was going to use the expression in the novel she was writing.

—What else have you written, she asked in a rather offhand way, as if she were not expecting an answer. And so I didn't answer. I know for a fact that she has only read a single book of mine and she probably didn't even finish it, although she claims to have written about it.

—Where? In which newspaper? Or which magazine?

—Not here, in Slovakia . . .

She asked me the question again, but this time she looked at me, smiling. And so I had to tell her something.

—I don't write . . . I don't feel like writing.

I was just about to add that I'm old, that at my age maybe I ought to stop aimlessly blackening reams of paper . . . But I had the strength to stop myself just in time. It also gets on Marianne's nerves to hear me moaning about being old all the time. I imagine it would get on her nerves even more . . . If I'm old, then I should just stay at home in my dressing gown and slippers reading the newspaper by the fireside.

—It's not important, she said, encouragingly. There's no point in writing all the time.

And she stroked my cheek. She had long, sharp nails, painted red.

—I'll get Pastenague to write . . . I said, attempting to make a joke. He's in top form . . .

—Who?

I explained to her who Pastenague was. He was born in

France, in Agen. He is younger than me, much younger, and eager to make a name for himself. His father was a jockey; he died under the horses' hooves during a steeplechase. His mother was a Romanian born and bred. I don't even think she was married to Pastenague the jockey, but she gave the child his surname, which was only natural given that he acknowledged it as his son. It's a French surname, from southwestern France, not a name from the back of beyond, from Romania. Ed Pastenague tried to become a writer, but nobody encouraged him on that path, an onerous one, it's true. My publisher can't stand him. I don't know what he's got against him, why he has such a grudge against him. I can't understand it. Lately, he has stubbornly refused to let his name appear on the cover of any book. He says that people haven't heard of him, as if anybody has heard of me. Tsepeneag, what, is that a name for a writer? Nobody can pronounce it. Not even in Romania . . . In Bucharest, when I telephone for a taxi, I prefer to give my name as Dumitru. You understand?

—But isn't it a Romanian name?

—I've no idea! Some say it comes from Hungarian, others claim it means something or other in Turkish . . .

—In Turkish?

—Yes, apparently it means lamb's wool, a lamb's wool coat . . . That's the meaning that has entered both Romanian and Hungarian.

—Have you looked it up in a Turkish dictionary?

—No, I haven't. Let the readers look it up . . . And the word *cioban* (shepherd) also comes from Turkish, and countless other words that we long believed to be Slavic. Not for nothing were we occupied by the Turks for almost three centuries.

—Three centuries! said Milena in astonishment, but also with compassion.

—Almost . . .

Right at that moment, a hedgehog entered the stage.

—Look, a hedgehog! cooed Milena, rising from her seat.

The hedgehog was moving quite quickly for a hedgehog. It was heading toward the middle of the stage. When it reached the pole, it stopped, turned to the audience and stood still for a few moments, twitching its muzzle. A fake blonde wearing a very short red skirt and a white silk blouse burst onto the stage, as if she'd been looking everywhere for the hedgehog. 'Here you are!' exclaimed the girl and knelt down by the hedgehog. She started scolding it, with her index finger outstretched. The hedgehog could have curled up into a ball, but it didn't; it endured the reproaches with dignity.

—I've been looking for you everywhere!

Nobody laughed.

There were just five or six people in the room, of which only one was a woman. True, it was a bit early for bona-fide striptease customers. Milena was looking for the waiter. She raised both arms in the air and shook them to attract his attention.

—I don't want champagne, she said to me.

—Nor do I . . .

The girl picked up the hedgehog, kissed it on the muzzle and went out, muttering something. The waiter was none too happy that we had ordered vodka. But he brought it all the same. Then, the girl came back onto the stage, but without the hedgehog, and started to undress.

I don't tell her about Milena, not because I am fearful of her jealousy—she has weathered other situations—but because I don't want to hear her sneering and asking me in a shrill voice:

—Who do you think you are, Kafka?

Best would be not to write to her for a while. But what do I do if she calls me on the telephone?

Well, I won't answer. As simple as that! I'll record a message informing her that I have gone to the countryside, at the invitation of my publisher. Let's say to Normandy. No, that won't work, Marianne knows him, she also probably has his mobile number, and she would be able to phone him. I have to come up with something else. Especially given that Milena also sometimes calls me on the telephone. Not very often, true. It's mostly I who call her on the mobile. I could tell her not to call me. But she'll ask me why . . .

I could tell them both that my mobile is broken. Or I could buy another one tomorrow, so that I have two numbers, one for each. The main thing will be not to get them mixed up . . .

she was walking down the middle of the street with short rapid steps it was as dark as in a forest she trod with quailing heart past lamp posts hunched like branchless leafless trees at first she hurried out of fear she felt like breaking into a run after a while the street abruptly went downhill and at the bottom a kind of valley seemed to open up outlined by the red light of the gibbous impotent sun that was slowly drowning in the sea yes there at the bottom was the sea of that there could be no doubt she was panting barefoot her feet sinking up to the ankles in sand first dry and loose then slightly moist dotted with seaweed from which rose the grinning head of now a lynx now a leopard and a little further on a she-wolf crossed her path but it was only the shadow that pierced her passed through her without flinching the fear had made her reckless for she couldn't stop now she was forced to keep going to run towards the huge iron gate that loomed threateningly next to the sea the long waves crawled like snakes jostling each other they rolled up the shore struck up against the iron gate with an inscription in Spanish or rather Italian in letters as big as daggers or swords the gate guarded on each side by a lion on which was inscribed something about hope

she stopped

in other words chuck it all down the toilet although she was next to the sea not merely the water in the bowl and a huge sow washed up like a wave-tossed sailing ship above all have no regrets if you're determined to pass through the gate it was cold and the wind was blowing more and more furiously

in the distance it was pitch black but still she thought to glimpse the outline of grey bodies moving chaotically back and forth probably naked arms reaching out elongating unnaturally in her direction beckoning her as if urging her to come to cross the threshold of the gigantic gate to enter to go among them to join them taking part in that enigmatic ballet

behind there now rose a mountain the colour of burnished brass like a bell whose summit was invisible because it was sliding closer and closer more and more threateningly in any event she no longer hoped to be able to return whence she came

she had no choice

with hesitant steps she crossed the threshold of the iron gate

and right away the darkness dissolved the naked bodies in front of her they now turned to an increasingly whitish or pinkish grey they were the same bodies that not long before had been beckoning her desperately but now they no longer paid her any heed they were wielding picks and shovels they were loading sand onto an enormous truck without being able to avoid the seaweed beyond the truck was the sea the waves of the sea that crashed furiously and came to a sudden stop mollified behind the toiling bodies

from time to time they stopped work and called out unintelligible words in a language probably a Slavic language but it wasn't Russian or Serbian Beatrice had had punters who when they reached the climax of excitement just before ejaculation muttered or even shouted in Russian that is what she believed without being at all sure of it but when she asked them where they were from some were Serbs or Czechs or Slovaks only once had she slept with a Bulgarian but he hadn't uttered a single word only mumbles

and once again the arms stretched out towards her they shoved each other fought each other they all wanted to touch her to clasp her body to grab her to squeeze her to rend her to tear her to pieces but they hampered each other and she began to retreat trying to reach the other side of the imposing arched gate to go back whence she came although she knew that it was not possible it was no longer possible she could already feel the arms the hands the nails which entered her flesh rent her tore away her skin flesh and all

she woke up panting and turned over on her other side with her face her nose pressed to the pillow

—I would like to send you what I have written up to now. So that you can give me your opinion.

—And then you'll hang up on me again . . .

—Forgive me: I lost my temper. But you ought to know that I took account of what you told me. I've even made some modifications.

—I'm glad!

—But I would like you to tell me what you think about how the plot is developing . . . I mean . . . you know . . .

Marianne hesitated for a few moments.

—I would rather read the whole thing in one sitting, from beginning to end. I don't like breaking off and then starting again and then stopping . . . You understand? Like that, there's no enjoyment . . .

—You're right. But it would help me if you had a quick look at this stage. After that, once it's been published, once the book is out, you can read it again, from start to finish.

—You mean I should read it twice?

—No, nobody is forcing you. Only if you want to. But it's now that I need your help . . .

For a time neither of us said anything. I was afraid to insist. I knew from experience that this was what annoyed her the most. I waited for her to make her mind up. She coughed, clearing her throat.

—All right, send me what you have written then . . . How much have you written?

—I don't know . . . About ninety pages. Maybe more.

—Don't you number the pages?

—No . . . I number them at the end.

—And how many pages do you intend to write?

—I've haven't got a clue! It depends . . .

—It depends on what?

—Well, if I'm in good form, if I like the result . . .

—Don't get started again. Don't go off on one of your long-winded rambles, like other things you've written, because nobody will read it.

—It's not as if anybody will read it anyway.

—You're making the effort for nothing, I'm telling you. Plus, you're not fifty years old any more . . . Nowadays nobody reads novels longer than two hundred pages. Even two hundred pages is long.

—But it's not a novel.

—Not a novel.

—No . . .

—Then what is it?

—I don't know what to call it. I've called it a *Building Site beneath the Open Sky*.

—Beneath the what?

—Beneath the open sky . . .

—What's that supposed to be?

—That's what it's called . . .

—I thought you said it was called *The Bulgarian Truck*.

—Yes . . . *The Bulgarian Truck*, and underneath, instead of 'a novel,' *Building Site . . .*

—*Beneath the Open Sky*?

—Well, yes . . .

—It's silly!

—You think?

—It's ridiculous!

—Who is Dimov? Milena asks me.

—A poet from last century.

—Russian or Bulgarian?

—Romanian.

—That's not a Romanian name.

—So what? . . . Almost everything he wrote was in Romanian.

—Yes, but I mean . . . all right. The Slavs had very close links to the Romanians.

I didn't say anything more. In that instant, the two of us were very close together: my left knee had found its way between her thighs, somewhere quite high up, where it was still very warm, hot even, after all the exercise we had just been doing together. She was sitting with her back to me, but I wasn't taking advantage. I was, if I can put it like this, taking a little breather. With my nose in her ear.

—Did you meet him?

I tried to answer as modestly as I could. But as I couldn't find the most suitable words, I murmured, the sounds emerging mostly through my nose:

—Yes, yes . . . Certainly . . .

—Did you ever talk to him?

—On occasion . . .

—Why don't you write poetry? Have you ever written poetry?

—No, not really. He used to write it on my behalf . . .

I might have added that poetry is more or less finished: it has lived its life; it has eaten its fill. But I didn't dare. I would have sounded a bit inappropriate, after my telling her about Dimov. Although I might have added that in fact Dimov didn't write poetry, but rather *texts*. I said the same thing back in the sixties, I wrote it in black and white, and at first Dimov was upset with me. In the end he understood it was positive . . .

In the end it was published anyway: *Les Frappes chirurgicales*. Paul felt sorry for the old author who hadn't published a book in at least three years. Now let's see if anybody will write about the book, anybody apart from, let's say, Corina.

—Your critics are dead, said Paul and there was no note of cynicism in how he put it.

It was a lucid assessment of the situation. Perhaps also sadness . . . Or regret. So I believe. Or to be more precise, nostalgia for the days when Gallimard didn't demand that he make a profit. Not Gallimard, I'm mistaken, back then P.O.L was owned by Flammarion.

The times were different . . . It's obvious that he's trying to avoid telling me that I have grown old and, given the 'jeunisme' of the present day, it's no wonder that in France my books get fewer and fewer reviews. I'm a kind of a throwback to the '70s, from before when the dictatorship set in . . . I mean the dictatorship of the public that demands young authors and beautiful authoresses. That demands the kind of literature that is suited to film adaptations, to American films, if not even television serials. Yes, sure, *Les Frappes* . . . it's a book of harsh, polemical criticism, it addresses a limited audience, but in order to be read even by this limited audience, it would have to have been written by a young writer. In which case it would have been seen as a rebellious, courageous, unsparing book, which gives a sound drubbing to all the stars of literary Paris. But as it is, having been written by an old codger, a non-entity, not French by birth but by adoption, it will be seen as a book by a failure, full of bitterness, envious of the success of the likes of Beigbeder, Anne Gavalda, Amélie Nothomb, and the other prominent writers he is shameless enough to mock. An alien has no right to such a book . . .

My critics are dead? Worse still is that I don't even have a translator since Alain fell ill.

We were at *Georges et Rosie*, furiously dancing the tango, when Milena announced that she was going away for a month or two, to her native Slovakia. She was wearing a short skirt that barely covered half her thighs. Her hair was dyed red and tied in a bun. She was smiling, revealing the dimple in her left cheek. She was beautiful.

—What are you going to do there?

She didn't answer right away. Her plump thigh was insistently touching my genitals. I had become aroused, the same as every other time. Probably that was what she was after. She liked it.

—I want to look for a publisher.

—Don't you have one?

—Yes, of course I do, but the one I've got is dissatisfied, he doesn't want us to go on like this.

—Why?

—Why what?

—Why is he dissatisfied?

—He's dissatisfied because he doesn't have the rights, but Gallimard.

—He's taking on Gallimard . . .

—He's not taking them on, but he says it doesn't suit him to publish me only in Slovakian, while Gallimard holds the translation rights for every other language . . .

—Naturally, given that you write in French. What translation rights anyway? Have you been translated in any other language than Slovak? And you translate yourself into Slovak.

She looks at me and laughs. The music stops. We are still holding hands and swaying from one leg to the other. She hasn't told me that her grandfather is seriously ill and that she wants to see him one last time. I discover that later.

—I'm not translated, but maybe I will be . . . You, for example, could translate me into Romanian.

I remained silent; I didn't know what to say. Apart from the dozen or so pages she read me one night, I hadn't read any of her books from start to finish. In other words, it was a shameless lie if I had somehow told her I had. No, I don't think I told her that. Maybe I just gave her to understand that I had read them. It's hardly the same thing . . . And anyway, had she read my books? So she claimed, but I had no proof. And what proof could I have? I could hardly subject her to an interrogation about the subjects and the characters. She would have sent me packing . . . Not to mention that I ran the risk of her asking me questions about her two novels. Only two? Three even, if you count the one she's writing . . .

So what if she hasn't read me! The naked truth is that writers don't much read each other's work. Especially when it comes to contemporaries, living writers. They're not curious. Is it that they are not interested or are they afraid of being influenced? I have no idea! Writers nowadays are hell bent on being original . . . I'm joking, of course. In fact I don't know what it is they want, apart from money. Success? They want to be liked by readers, but also by the critics. And so possibly they read reviews of the latest books. Their own, obviously, and perhaps other writers' . . .

I leaned forward and kissed her on the mouth, and she gladly joined in. She had a way of kissing that was all her own: she stuck out her lower lip, which was fleshy, strong, and sucked your lips, your whole mouth. It was a delight . . .

Then, the music started up again. In one corner of the room I glimpsed the head of a piglet. But I was probably only imagining it.

he was driving through a village of very squat blue yellow and green houses with diminutive inhabitants who were minding their own business which is to say they were hanging clothes on lines they didn't bother to look at that van that had pretensions to being a truck and which was speeding down that lane without sidewalks clothes of every colour were dancing gaily in the breeze then the truck reached the end of the village he abruptly found himself in a forest the road narrowed it was getting narrower and narrower and the light was getting dimmer and dimmer but he could still make out small animals like squirrels although they weren't squirrels they looked more like seahorses they hopped around in front of the truck or made all kinds of leaps flying from one tree to another

naturally the truck was no longer driving over asphalt or even over beaten or muddy earth but over sand in front of him he could no longer see the trees but only water it was a lake or perhaps even the sea and so he had to brake in order not to end up in the water but he pressed the brake pedal in vain the sea was getting closer and closer the waves were visible through the window which was misted for some reason they were getting higher and higher Tsvetan jerked the steering wheel to the right and pulled the hand brake screeching from every join the truck came to a stop a few metres from the water almost parallel with the sea with the waves that were climbing higher and higher and seemingly they were no longer waves Tsvetan turned on the windscreen wipers and so now he could see clearly the huge snakes that were emerging from the sea they were snakes not waves they were undulating pushing against each other but they did not remain on the shore they returned with a motion lent perfect rhythm probably by the sea currents or by somebody or other lurking far away over the horizon

Marianne on the telephone again:

—What are you up to? Aren't you going to send me the novel?

—What novel?

—*The Bulgarian Truck.*

—It's not a novel . . .

—Yes, well, whatever you want to call it. A text . . . A text beneath the cloud-covered sky.

I say nothing. She's making fun of me: this is all I need! Why did I have to start on about literary theory? In the first place, theory in general gets on her nerves. Matchstick theory, as she likes to call it: don't give me your two-bit theories! To her, theory, if not deleterious, is in any case superfluous. And critical jargon annoys her even more, all those terms that seem to say more than they actually do and which she has to look up in the dictionary, and sometimes can't even find them there. I don't know what possessed me to go on and on to her about a novel I'd barely started, and above all to tell her about the title and the subtitle . . . But now, if I strike out the word *novel*, it doesn't mean that I stand any greater chance of gaining her approval. On the contrary.

Beneath a cloud-covered sky . . . If I think about it, it's not a bad title. I like it. I'll think about it . . .

—Hello! Hello!

—Yes.

—Why don't you answer?

—I do answer, but you didn't ask me anything.

—Yes I did. I asked you why you haven't sent me that nonsense beneath the something or other sky.

—I'll send you it, but I have to work on it some more.

—You said you needed advice. Before finishing it. That's what you told me a few days ago. Afterwards, I'm warning you, it will be too late.

—I do need advice, but I haven't solved the problem of punctuation.

—You're having problems with punctuation?

—I've always had problems with punctuation.

—What kind of problems?

—I haven't decided whether it would be better not to leave any punctuation . . .

—Again? Without any punctuation? The same as in *The Something-or-other Wedding*?

—Not the whole text: some passages with and some without.

—I don't understand. I won't understand unless I see it. Send me it as it is and I'll see.

She's right. Literature should be read, it's not enough for it to be described, commented on, analysed, if it's not read.

And it's even better that it can be done at first hand, not like in music, through performers. Literature may resemble music, as I like to claim, but it's not quite music: if you can't hear it, it doesn't exist . . . True, it's sufficient for a musician to see the score. Therefore, music can also be read. Deciphered . . . I don't know; it's complicated.

In the Metro. A conversation between two old writers obsessed with the imperilment of memory . . . One of them is bald and has grown a beard to make up for it. He looks like a politician, I forget his name, which is normal given that I can no longer watch him on television . . . He used to be a regular guest of Denisot on Canal Plus. In the evening, prime time. Since then it's as if he died. The politician, I mean . . . The other writer was wearing a black bowtie and a pink shirt. He was holding in both hands an umbrella with a parrot-head handle. A yellow one.

I heard them talking in the Metro. Yes, yes, with my own ears, I heard them. And I saw them . . . I mean to say that the scene is not an invention. It's a slice of life, as they say when publicising a book, in the hope of attracting as large an audience as possible, since it is well known that the public adores slices brimming with life, as juicy as slices of melon . . .

— . . . you haven't published in a while.

—Um, right . . .

—You've haven't the time to write. I understand. You know, I too . . .

—No, I do have the time. I work almost every day. It's all I do. But as for reading, I don't read anymore. I just write . . . But I'm not satisfied with the result. So I erase it, make it vanish . . . The *ordinateur* is perfect for doing that. I don't even know whether I should say that it helps me or on the contrary . . .

—You're not the only one in that situation.

—That's right . . . but it's no consolation. I'm afraid lest I write a book that is, you know, superfluous.

—We write superfluous books, regardless. It doesn't depend on us. I think you'll agree . . .

—What do you mean?

—I mean that it isn't we who decide whether a book is superfluous or not. Or even which books . . . Maybe all of them are superfluous. We can't know anything beforehand.

—You're right, but admit that we have more chances of writing a superfluous book now, at the end of our game, than at the beginning. The first book can't be superfluous, because it's the first.

—Do you think the last is superfluous anyway, just because it's the last?

—That's not what I meant.

I have to admit I didn't find the conversation enthralling. But they went on talking and willy-nilly I went on listening. I couldn't hardly get off the train before my station and nor could I put my fingers in my ears . . .

They got on to the subject of memory.

— . . . afraid that I'll forget it by the next morning, I get up in the middle of the night and write it down and after that I can't get back to sleep. I toss and turn, I twist around from one side to the other, but in vain! I can't get back to sleep. That is, I sleep four or five hours a night. Which would be no great loss—as it is I sleep too much!

—We're a weary species, a somnolent species . . .

—Yes, but after that I feel sleepy the whole day, I'm useless. How am I supposed to write under such conditions?

—Take sleeping pills.

—It's dangerous. You know very well that if you get used to sleeping pills, you're shackled with them after that. And they wear out your memory. Some even say that sleeping pills hasten the onset of that incurable illness. You know the one . . .

—I've heard that too.

—Already my memory is not what it used to be.

—A chess player's memory!

—It's gone . . . I don't play chess anymore. In any case, a chess player has a special kind of memory. It's a special compartment of the memory. Chess doesn't help you with anything, certainly not with writing.

—A pity . . .

—Now, if I think of a scene or a dialogue while I'm stewing

in the sheets, I don't want to get up. It's barely struck midnight and I'd like to get some sleep, but the next day I realise that I've forgotten almost everything. Before, I used to write entire pages in my head. Once I was on a train, I was travelling to Vienna and I didn't have a pencil or paper on me . . .

—I always keep a notebook on the bedside table and a luminous pen, you know, one that also serves as a flashlight . . .

—Interesting . . .

—That way I don't disturb my wife.

—Do you sleep in the same bed with her?

—Yes, she won't have it any other way. I tried to persuade her, but I didn't succeed.

—There, you see, that's no good. Take me, if I wake up, I make an effort, I turn on the light, I go to my office and I start writing, I mean I try to write. Since I no longer have any faith in my memory . . .

—And what does your wife say?

—She doesn't say anything. She died last year.

—Ah, yes. Forgive me.

—No harm done.

as a child she had done a little ballet Victor used to take her by the hand every week on Wednesdays when she didn't have school it helped her in her later career

she gripped the pole and began to spin around hanging first by both arms then by one arm true she was a little afraid at one point she attempted a special number she unbuttoned her blouse with just one hand while still spinning around and she didn't have a bra she also tried it with a bra but it was much too difficult to hold on to the bar and at the same time to unfasten that stupid clasp since she never understood what was the point of it and her well-proportioned breasts didn't need any support they were like pears somewhat bigger they looked like the tits of the *Venus of Urbino* yes the woman in the Titian painting she saw in the Louvre she was alone not with Danet

once she was down to just her panties she stopped spinning around true it was about time because she had grown dizzy she stopped and with the required slowness she began to take them off the music stopped all eyes were fixed on her belly button on the pelt she refused to shave off and they all discovered with delight how black and bushy it was like the beard of a dwarf hiding inside her fofoloancă

Danet would laugh agitatedly every time and could barely restrain himself from rushing over to her

I hadn't seen Alain since his operation. Now he was at home. He had been terribly gaunt when he got back from the hospital. A skeleton. He could barely speak. His voice was feeble, gasping. It was no longer the voice it used to be: a clear, baritone voice, with perfect diction. A radio announcer's voice. It was as if a different person was now living inside him . . .

He spent his days eating, in the kitchen, or rather trying to eat, because he couldn't really manage it. For that reason it took him a long time . . . He had difficulty swallowing. Even liquids. Every time he swallowed it entailed pain and effort. In any case, you couldn't really say he was eating, but rather he drank, as he was unable to chew. But nor did he always manage to drink. He would choke. He would cough. Sometimes he would go to the sink to spit. I tried to pretend I was unaffected by it. At first, I didn't ask him any questions about the operation. I didn't realise that this was precisely what he wanted to talk about. About the operation and the illness in general. In fact, for as long as I was there, around two hours, he talked only about himself. About his illness. He wasn't complaining; he described the symptoms, the pains. In vain did I try to turn the subject to other matters. Out of politeness, he let me talk, but it was obvious he wasn't interested. His mind was elsewhere.

Tristan was at school. That day, he decided to go to pick him up. The school is a stone's throw from the building where Alain lives. We went together.

I woke up at the crack of dawn I was experiencing a feeling of well-being I had been dreaming about writing a novel without punctuation all I had to do was add a few full stops and commas at the end when I finished it I was writing quickly it was as if it were typing itself on the keyboard of the *ordinateur* and the novel about the Bulgarian truck was rolling along smoothly Tsvetan was whistling at the steering wheel with his umbrella by his side the one whose handle was shaped like a crow's head but let's not get carried away it was more like a hawk's head an eagle's head with a curved very sharp beak

then the road was blocked by a building site what I mean is that the road was under repair Tsvetan braked but the truck didn't stop dead but skidded for another few metres a good job he pulled the hand brake and he managed to come to a stop just half a metre behind a red car which had probably come to a stop because of another car which had probably

he even dented it a little what the hell it happens

that was how he met Daisy at the petrol station a few kilometres further down the road Tsvetan had pulled into the petrol station to check his engine his hand brake which didn't seem to be working properly Daisy was in the red car she came after him and started speaking to him in English the Bulgarian had learned English at the American high school he used to say that he was more interested in English than any other subject he was already thinking of becoming a truck driver when Sonia heard him she would get annoyed

get some sense into your head Sonia would say and he couldn't understand why she used to get so annoyed about it

what do you want me to do learn French and become a writer

and so he could get along quite well in English he had had the opportunity to practice during his trips all over Europe everybody was capable of stringing a few words together in that genuinely international language

Daisy wanted to ask his advice on the best way to get to Podgorica he didn't waste time thinking about it he told her the easiest thing would be to follow his truck it wasn't all that far they would get there in no time she was American not English all right then Tsvetan thought about saying something to her about Bush and how much people admired him in Bulgaria and not only in Bulgaria but in all the other surrounding former communist states and especially in Romania where Tsvetan had been recently with a mysterious load contained in sealed crates which nobody had even inspected at the border then he changed his mind he remembered that Bush wasn't going to be in office much longer there was going to be an election the American woman looked anxious probably impatient and so he climbed into the cab of his truck Daisy was following just ten metres behind smiling to herself for some unknown reason

two hours later they reached Podgorica

I have sent the opening pages to Marianne. Rather premature, she said when I told her over the telephone that she'd be receiving them soon. Lately, I've given up trying to find out whether she is being ironic or not. For obvious reasons, I omitted the pages where I wasn't able to substitute Milen for Milena. I also skipped a number of passages about Beatrice, which she might have found too lubricious. I don't know whether I did a good thing or not . . . Having done so, having concealed a part of the text from her, I'm not sure what point there is in asking for her opinion. I regret it now, but it's too late. Although it has to be said that she has less to read like this.

—It's a pity you don't have an *ordinateur* with an Internet connexion at your end.

—What possible use would I have for one?

—We could communicate more easily . . .

Just three days later she telephones me again.

—What? You've received it already? I say in simpleminded astonishment.

—The U.S. Postal Service is quick.

—Yes, well . . . So . . . have you read it?

—Yes, of course I've read it.

—It's not the final draft, you do realise. There are a few places where I can add or, on the contrary, subtract things. It's a building site . . .

—Thank the Lord!

—What do you mean?

—Here's what . . . I'm saying it for your own good. I don't want you to get upset. You know very well that I always try to be sincere when I'm giving my opinion. This is why you need my opinion. You know that I don't lie. And this is not the first time I've told you . . .

—Say what you've got to say!

—You ought not to write novels anymore.

—But what should I write?

—Short stories.

—I wrote enough short stories in my youth.

—Or sketches . . . Texts of two or three pages. Or better still, poems. Really short poems, haikus . . .

—You're exaggerating!

—Of course I'm exaggerating. In order to be more convincing.

—But what's your criticism? Specifically . . .

—It's full of repetitions.

—Repetitions?

—Yes, yes . . .

—That's the way I write . . . It's musical! Don't you know?

—I think you're exaggerating on that point, with the music . . . Your poor unfortunate reader. He'll get the impression that he's always reading the same text. That he's going round in circles . . .

—Good.

—He'll think that you've forgotten what you've already written and that's why you have written it again. Or that you were in a hurry and bungled the job. The reader isn't going to think of music . . . He bought a novel. He paid money for a book because he likes literature, not music. Understand? Why put him out? If he wants music, he'll listen to music . . . He'll buy himself some records or CDs. He'll go to a concert. It's that simple.

—Yes, it's simple.

—The novel is the art of complexity, as the great Milan Kundera said. But it's not music . . .

—I see you're repeating yourself . . .

—I'm repeating myself so that you'll get it into your head.

I say nothing. There is nothing else I can do. I'm of course tempted to hang up the telephone, but I restrain myself. In the end, wasn't I the one who sent her the manuscript? Wasn't I the one who asked for her opinion and insisted that she should read it now that I have reached, at best, the midway point of the novel?

After a brief pause, she goes back on the attack:

—For Beatrice, the Beatrice character . . . couldn't you have found a less pompous name for her? I mean . . .

—The names can be changed.

—. . . I mean. And another thing, you make this Beatrice—or whatever her name is—blonde on one page and brunette on the next.

—Really? I hadn't noticed.

—You hadn't noticed because you're a senile old fool. I told you not to write another novel . . .

—Here you go again . . . If you're right, then thank you for drawing my attention to it and for helping me out like this . . .

—There, you see . . .

—But the reader might imagine that she dyes her hair: first black, then blonde.

—Why not white?

—You're right. White would be even more exciting. Black/white. In fact it's a natural alternation . . .

—You're being facetious! You would be better off playing chess, even though you've never been any great shakes at chess, either. At least at chess the verdict isn't long and drawn-out . . . You lost, now sling your hook! Whereas in literature you can believe you're no end of a good thing . . . You imagine that the people who criticise you don't have any idea about modern, I beg your pardon, about postmodern literature . . . An utterly stupid idea, you must admit . . .

I have hung up the telephone on her. Yet again.

Angrily, I sit down in front of the *ordinateur*. I look for the offending passages and delete them. For example: 'have you seen his biceps his pectorals his shoulders his dark eyes and his greasy skintight trousers stretched over his muscular thighs so that his genital organ stands out in relief more prominently than in other men women are sensitive to such external signals . . .' It's pointless my getting annoyed. Like a fool. Maybe Marianne is right. As far as music goes . . . There's no need to go over the top. I'm not going to turn my novel into a kind of Ravel's *Bolero*. Apart from anything else, the composition would be too simple. Too simplistic . . .

When it comes to Beatrice's hair colour, my patience runs out before I find the passage in question and so I give up.

on the first few days the customers thronged to her door

they pushed and shoved they darted each other venomous looks so impatient were they to meet her the word was out that she was hard to penetrate but in time that fact which had aroused the curiosity of some drove away many more because it seemed to them a kind of humiliation not to be able to penetrate her not to mention the money that they forked out for nothing and so her clients dwindled but they were loyal and enthusiastic why not say proud to be among those who had succeeded they formed a kind of club an Englishmen who thought he was funny dubbed it the Woodcock Association I don't know whether he was a member . . .

Danet increased the fee but he still saw it as a losing proposition he earned less with Beatrice than he did with the other girls who were far from having her class but they could be penetrated with ease and finished the job more quickly much more quickly

he tried to offset the loss by selling all kinds of ointments designed to smooth the way there was a special room for this trade in ointments meant for Beatrice but it was still hopeless no matter how many ointments he sold

one evening a client entered her having made stubborn and strenuous efforts but then the necessary ointment ran out and because he was too niggardly to buy another his organ remained trapped

penis captivus is something that happens very rarely and the more the poor man pulled desperately trying to get out the more she contracted and the walls of her vagina clamped his schlong like a vice

kiss my breasts cried Beatrice suck them bite them . . .

she was moving in every direction contorting herself trying desperately to extrapolate herself but in vain her cries could be heard in the adjoining rooms the boss himself arrived the hulking Danet he grasped the client by the arse and tried to drag him out another client arrived who claimed to be a doctor he was wearing only his long johns

penis captivus penis captivus

Beatrice was weeping the client was cursing his head off and demanding his money back

what is needed is an injection said the doctor who still hadn't had time to pull his trousers up what injection said another there were by now a number of them around the bed poke a finger up her arse it's easier each was voicing his own opinion pour cold water over them both

Beatrice didn't remain at the Vertige d'amour for long after that Danet didn't try to sleep with her anymore and so he fired her after a while she was forced to sign on as unemployed again

'Trop de sexe tue le sexe,' so said Marianne, in French, although she is living in New York. And when you think that I excised a whole load of sex scenes from the pages I sent her. For example, what Beatrice got up to in bed with the girl from Martinique; I described their embraces in great detail, using rather crude language. Or a part of Tsvetan's adventures on his travels through Europe, given that he hardly led the life of a monk. But I left in the bit with him and Daisy, otherwise the character would have run the risk of becoming unrealistic.

At times Marianne can be right . . . Maybe I ought to tone down some words, present the love scenes in a more poetic light. There is one thing poetry is good for at least . . . So, there should be more suggestiveness and less description. Or else I should just leave certain actions in the penumbra.

But no matter, before I send the text to my publisher I have all the time in the world to hack it down to size. To castrate it, as it were . . . Or to add to it: to graft new scenes onto it, to insert sentences and words, even to alter it here and there.

—Take me with you to Slovakia, I told Milena during our last night of love in Paris.

Milena looked at me as if she were seeing me for the first time. A look that seemed to me ironic, although I wasn't very sure. On my part, it was like a declaration of love, but how should I say? she took it literally. Physically. Geographically. She was probably picturing herself in public with me in Bratislava: with an old minor writer who doesn't even know Czech, pardon, Slovak or Russian. Or even English. Not to mention that she would probably be going accompanied . . . Or was someone waiting for her there, an old flame? The fact that she is published in Paris (by Gallimard no less!), that she writes in French could hardly leave the young Slovak intellectuals of her generation unmoved.

I remember one day we were both at a café in the Place Saint-Suplice. It was quite rare for us to go out together, usually we met in her one-room flat. And a tall, handsome young man appeared, he looked like that Serb or Croat tennis player—what the hell is his name? Djokovic or something of the sort. He came straight up to our table. He was as supple and smiling as a tiger that has just espied a gazelle and is moving towards it. Rather embarrassed, Milena introduced us. He was a Czech photographer. She introduced me as a writer published by Gallimard. 'Like myself,' she added, smiling from ear to ear. The photographer sat down at our table, ordered a beer, and from time to time spoke to Milena in Czechoslovak.

She stroked my brow. She whispered to me, in a gentle, almost pitying voice:

—Another time, my darling. Another time . . .

—I was joking, I said haughtily.

And I said the wrong thing. I ought to have said that it was in fact a declaration of love. But I didn't. I fell silent. And she fell silent, continuing to stroke my brow, mechanically; I could feel her touch growing lighter, her fingers becoming more and more inattentive. We can sometimes betray ourselves without words. Nor are words always a good thing; we don't always hit the target, sometimes it's even worse. For example, what possessed me to tell her this:

—I'm leaving too. I'm going to New York.

Ought we to be afraid of the Bulgarian truck driver?

In the 2005 European referendum campaign, the role of the Polish plumber was to frighten those who wanted enlargement of the European Union. A symbol of excessive liberalisation, within a few months the plumber had vanished. Nowadays, a new bogeyman has appeared. It's no longer a question of the man who repairs our pipes, but the man who transports them.

Philippe de Villiers has found a new anti-European bogeyman for his election campaign. This time it is the Bulgarian truck driv-

er, who apparently sleeps only four hours a night and eats only twice a week. He is a terrible menace to French hauliers. But where the hell did De Villiers come up with this Bulgarian truck driver?

According to Patrick Louis, the Mouvement Pour La France MEP, the Eurosceptics discovered him in a car park in Marseilles.

'Fifteen days ago, Philippe De Villiers and myself were in Marseilles in the car park of a road haulage company that was laying off workers because of Bulgarian truck drivers. We were told that a Spanish truck, driven in shifts by two Bulgarian drivers, was making the return journey between the factory in Aubagne and the warehouses in Marseilles twenty-four hours a day nonstop, delivering cans of Coca-Cola.'

Nicolas Poulssen, the deputy general of the National Federation of Road Hauliers, refuses to bandy about the peril of the 'Bulgarian truck driver,' but nor is he surprised that Philippe De Villiers can't refrain from doing so.

'The Government made no efforts to prepare for this change. They came to their senses just twenty-four hours before the newcomers received haulage licences. And all they did then was to request a six-month extension of the temporary measure to protect us.'

In Bulgaria the minimum wage is 110 *Euros a month. And so it is understandable that French businesses prefer the Bulgarian truck driver. Even if he doesn't have a haulage licence, there is nothing to prevent a Bulgarian truck driver from coming to France and finding work at a very competitive wage. In any event, since* 2006 *Brussels has allowed employees to work 'temporarily' in any other country in accordance with the social and wage regulations of their native country.*

*(*No Way, *June 2009)*

—How is that Slovenian of yours?

—What Slovenian?

—The writer . . . Milan or whatever his name is.

—He's from Slovakia, not Slovenia, I said, stickler for accuracy that I am.

—Slovakia, Slovenia, same difference.

—How is he? He's writing . . . Reading . . . Why ask me? Is that why you called me, just to ask me this?

—In fact I telephoned you to say that I've sent you a photograph in an attachment. A surprise. I went to a cybercafé especially. I sent you it two days ago, but I see you've had no reaction. Or haven't you switched on your *ordinateur*?

—I haven't switched it on.

—What about the novel?

—I'm writing it by hand . . . I'm making notes, that is. I've come up with some new characters. I don't know whether to keep the old ones. I've half a mind to start writing a different novel, a real novel, that is.

—What kind of novel?

—I don't know . . . Maybe a novel about love . . .

For a few seconds Marianne doesn't say anything. Then she erupts:

—I'm sick of your novels about love. They all get stuck at the planning stage. Which is hardly surprising. You haven't got a clue about what love is . . . Egotist that you are, you're not even capable of imagining what it is. Drop it! God knows what the result will be . . . And besides, you promised Paul that you'd finish the one about the Bulgarian first.

—Paul couldn't give a shit about my books.

—Don't take it like that . . . You're being unfair! I get the impression that your ships have all sunk . . . We'll talk about it some other time. And now you're getting angry over nothing . . .

—It wasn't me who . . .

—All right, drop it! Why not switch on the *ordinateur* instead and look at the photograph I sent you.

I didn't have any choice. I switched it on. I connected to the Internet, I looked in my inbox, I clicked on the attachment, and what did I see: a photograph in which Marianne is smiling from ear to ear, and next to her is a young woman who looks familiar . . . But I can't put a name to the face.

—Who is it? The person . . . I say, awkwardly.

—What, don't you recognise Laura, my friend from New York? It was you who said that you'd do all kinds of things to her, because you liked her so much.

—I would even now . . . I boasted.

—Didn't you recognise her?

—Not at first, although it seemed to me I'd seen that pretty little face of hers somewhere before. Now I recognise her, of course. She looks like she's put on weight. Her body, I mean . . . She's developed . . . Her breasts are twice as big.

—And what's wrong with that?

—Nothing's wrong. I mean. I like slightly smaller breasts, otherwise there's a danger of their sagging, of their drooping.

—How can you talk like that about the girl's breasts! You're talking nonsense . . . Laura has superb breasts.

—She's wearing clothes, a bra, I can't tell . . .

I could sense Marianne getting more and more annoyed. Maybe Laura was right there next to her, or within earshot, and she could hear what we were nattering about or at least guess from what Marianne was saying. I was putting her in rather an awkward situation. It was clear that she was in no mood for jokes, although she was trying to remain amiable and even playful, which was further proof she was not alone. Making an effort, with rather a grating laugh, she flung at me:

—Maybe you'd like her naked? On a leopard skin . . .

Yes, I would.

Whichever way you look at it, old age also has something downright ridiculous about it. I'm not saying it's grotesque. It's also grotesque, towards the end, but it's a grotesqueness that quickly becomes tragic. It's perceived as being grotesque but rarely and not for long. It engenders empathy. I'm therefore trying to say that it's not only tragic . . . It's also ridiculous. Before being grotesque and becoming tragic, it's perceived as ridiculous. By others, but also by ourselves. This impression might also arise because in fact we are not prepared to experience it.

In childhood, after a given point, that is, after we have passed the paradisiacal age, which usually comes to an end at around the age of four or five, all we do is to prepare ourselves for adult life: we go to school, we acquire knowledge that is of no use to us at the time (true, it isn't of much use in adolescence either, nor later even . . .), we are almost obsessed with the maturity that awaits us. Both we and those around us. We are preparing for life! As if the rest—for example all that time we spend in school—were not life . . .

But what about old age? How do we prepare for that? Not only don't we prepare for it, but we do everything we can to deny it. We want to look young, in top form, we resort to all kinds of cures and medical advice, we pretend it doesn't even exist, that it can't touch us. This is where the ridiculous comes in. 'The country is ablaze and the old woman is combing her hair,' here is a proverb which, to me, also expresses the following: life is slipping by and we refuse to take heed. I do admit, this model of thought is quite simple, if not simplistic, even. Ultimately, what are we to do? Death ripples around old age, we are swimming towards nothingness . . . I say 'swimming' because we are subjected to an increasingly strenuous daily effort. Would it be better if we posed as victims? If we sighed and moaned from dawn to dusk? I'm not sure even about that.

Alain is ill, he has throat cancer and even though they say that this type of cancer is not metastatic, to me at least it seems obvious that he does not have long to live. But nonetheless, he doesn't like it if I commiserate with him. Even though after the operation, which wasn't a great success, he must have been in terrible suffering. And likewise now, after chemotherapy. But he doesn't complain. He doesn't even want to see many people. Sometimes you get the impression that he hasn't lost hope of surviving the illness. Fear and hope prop each other up . . .

Daisy smiled at him and told him to come to her hotel
with the truck

but you won't be sleeping in the truck said the American woman

I'm used to it

that may be but it's still better in a bed

he laughed and parked his truck on a side street not far from the hotel

Daisy couldn't keep her eyes off him a little later in the restaurant during dinner and he reached under the table with his arm and without further ado he stroked her thighs with the palm of his hand they were thick, meaty

you're in a rush she said and she almost choked on her soup

after another two or three mouthfuls she put her spoon down she got up from the table come on let's go but he calmly went on eating

I'm in no hurry and he ordered a rare steak

the night was long and full of adventures each more pleasant than the next not counting the truck driver's premature ejaculation these things happen especially the first time but he quickly made up for it after that and not even the fellatio interrupted because the Bulgarian's organ didn't seem to fit in the American's buccal cavity or perhaps it was nothing but her unfounded fear as she didn't have much experience however I cannot but mention that the bed was squeaking horrendously and the people in the adjoining room were complaining that they couldn't sleep and they were banging on the wall in desperation but how can you ask Tsvetan to stop now just when he's enjoying himself and Daisy had ended up with her feet on the headboard of the bed right next to the fist on the other side of the wall banging away to no avail

the night was long and every corner of the room served as a venue for the pleasure-inflamed bodies of the couple by morning they were embracing in the bathroom in the water-filled tub or next to it

Daisy had got used to the size and ardour of Tsvetan she had acquired a taste for him and she would have been capable of keeping it up for who knows how long

An e-mail from Milena: '*I miss you.*'

That's all.

When we parted, she was rather cold.

—I'm not being cold, she said, it's just the way I am ... Never mind, I'll write to you, don't worry.

She knew my address, of course, as we had already exchanged a few anodyne e-mails, about books, but nothing more. In Paris we made love, but we didn't talk about the feelings that might accompany such acts aimed at bringing that sensation of pleasure desired by any couple.

'*I miss you.*'

It might have remained a mere fling, I wasn't hoping for

anything more, especially given that the age difference between us is indeed great. What else might I have been hoping for? This is probably what I shall write to her about, if I write to her. And of course I'm going to write to her . . .

News in brief

Yesterday at around 17:30, on national road 164, at the exit to the Plemet bypass, there was a fatal collision between a car and a truck. The truck driver, a Bulgarian national, was unable to avoid the car coming from the opposite direction. In the vehicle was a young woman of 24, who was injured, but not seriously, and taken to the hospital in Loudeac.

I miss you: this is what she wrote to me. And what should I reply to her? Because I can't not write to her; I don't have the strength not to. And ultimately, what good would it do me? True, I don't have to reply to her right away . . .

But I could only hold out until the next day. At the crack of dawn, wearing my pyjamas, I rushed to switch on the *ordinateur* and began to write:

The e-mail is the weapon of the poor man, the faraway man, the blind man . . . It's pointless our writing words if we can't see each other. I stretch out my arms and you're not there. The only thing left for me to do is to write to you. To write? Not even the song of songs would be of any use.

Before you left you were a little ice floe. An ice cube: but don't put it in your whiskey. I told myself: she is conducting our love and lowering her baton so that I, and the whole orchestra inside me, will stop the deafening crescendo. Subdue the instruments before they go off the rails, before they get out of time and the music turns into a cacophony. That's what I told myself.

You went away. I'm left by myself . . .

My head is full of you. Your body is in my head: your left leg sticks out of my left ear, your right leg out of my right ear. And your body and your head are in my head . . . Then why can't I decipher what you're telling me? What does it mean that you miss me?

I hesitated for a long while. Mightn't what I wrote be a little exaggerated? Strained metaphors. Obviously, she's hardly going to take them literally. She is a writer after all. But perhaps herein lies the mistake, in treating an incipient amour in an excessively literary way. Or what else might I call it? I let myself be carried away by the keyboard of the *ordinateur*, as if carried away on the waves. I didn't even venture the slightest hint of irony. Or a joke . . .

Should I delete it and write another e-mail? I don't have the courage. Nor the inclination. I don't know how she will react to it, but I hope that she'll understand that it isn't easy to break free of the conventions of the genre. A love letter is still a love letter . . . Maybe it's not the case to talk about being overly literary: exaggeration is intrinsic; it's part of the concept. But is what exists between us really love?

I continued with the cheap philosophising like that for a number of minutes. In the end I don't know who it was (maybe Pastenague . . .) who hit 'send,' and the e-mail set off into thin air.

I have never understood and nor will I ever understand how an *ordinateur* works: modern technology is beyond me; it humbles me.

A quarter of an hour later, I received her e-mail:

I know: I was awful. I was trying to conduct an orchestra, that much is true, but it wasn't yours, it was mine. And coldness comes off quite well for me, because when I am experiencing something very intense, I become paralysed.

'I miss you' means that I would give anything to reach out and touch you. It also means that what is to come will verge on the unbearable. You really must come to Prague.

She has joined in the game . . . It's obvious. Now what do I do? Do I plunge giddily into the whole story? . . . Maybe this is what she wants in fact: for me really to fall in love with her and therefore she is exaggerating her feelings. But haven't I been going about it the same way? Doesn't my e-mail rest under the sign of exaggeration? The question is whether this exaggeration in any way corresponds to a real feeling, whether I have been exaggerating in order to get a feeling across. The same doubt is valid for both of us . . . Otherwise it's nothing but *ordinateur* literature! I don't think the same words would have come out of my mouth if we'd been face to face. It's also easier via the *ordinateur* than it is over the telephone. Easier and therefore more dangerous . . .

Ordinateur literature will replace train-station reading, it will spread from one continent to another, by land and sea, internauts will tell the stories of their loves and dreams to each other. They will make friends, they will fall in love e-mailing from Montreal to Melbourne, from Los Angeles to Satu Mare. They don't need to see each other face to face. Nor do they need to believe in their words. The whole world will turn into a bubble of sentimental fiction.

after she left the Vertige d'amour for a week she didn't leave the house except two or three times to buy herself something to eat she was dazed by what had happened to her she lay stretched out on the bed staring at the ceiling she couldn't even be bothered to get dressed she lay in just her pyjama top or a thin see-through nightie viewing her from above let's say from the light fixture on the ceiling you cannot help but admire her absolutely superb body

one fine day when the sun was shining and the sky was blue she got dressed and went out of the house for a walk she wandered at random looking vacantly in the shop windows she didn't have a destination and she found herself on a street where there was a bookshop and where a year before or longer they had been doing some major excavations nobody knew what the excavations were for or why they took as long as they did in the end the work stopped now there was almost no trace of it the holes or rather the ditches had been filled in the pavement had been put back no trace of any digging here and there the cobblestones were askew the only clue to point to the excavations and indirectly to what had happened there in the hole and the diggers had vanished tools and all as if the earth had swallowed them perhaps it never really happened that which she believed had happened

she stopped in front of a bookshop which she remembered

perfectly well she could swear it was the same bookshop from the time of the excavations on the pavement where she stopped to gawp at the diggers

she went inside the bookshop

distrait she flicked through the books displayed on the counter she pretended to be interested and one by one she took the books off the shelves opened them turned a few of the pages with her finger suddenly jerked her head towards the page as if she couldn't believe her eyes and then closed them and put them back

are you looking for any book in particular a fat bookseller asked her removing the ballpoint pen from behind his ear and starting to fiddle with it in front of Beatrice and she didn't know what to say luckily she recalled the title of a book she had not got around to reading *Through the Keyhole* or something of the sort

the title doesn't sound familiar is it a novel

I don't know exactly I don't think so in any case the author didn't give it a subtitle

I'm not talking about the subtitle said the bookseller getting annoyed is it or isn't it a novel

if it's not a novel then what else could it be asked Beatrice cowed

it might be a collection of poems or essays it might be a lot of things

I don't think it's a novel whispered Beatrice and added in a whisper they're not digging anymore

pardon

a while ago they were digging on this street weren't they in front of the bookshop I mean

the bookseller whacked himself mercilessly across the fingers with his ballpoint pen he didn't seem to understand what she was talking about

excavations

yes there were deep ditches and diggers with picks and shovels they were digging from dawn to dusk stripped to the waist in the sun I assure you

the bookseller said nothing he gazed through the bookshop window outside on the street there were no passersby it was a quiet street rarely did you see a passing car from time to time a cyclist would pass looking left and right as if he had got lost he didn't know where he was for that reason the book trade was slowly dying out soon the bookshop would have to close down there was a rumour that it would be sold to be converted into a pharmacy although a colleague claimed that the premises were going to be transformed into a funeral parlour

Olivia is a gigantic sow on the seashore
I'm writing without punctuation in dreams there are no commas
and even less so any full stops
just capital letters from time to time as big as Olivia
the total sow
the goddess of love
as round as the letter O
emerging from the radioactive seaweed
she comes slowly towards me and I feel
terrified and tempted at the same time
I stiffen
I gradually sink into the wet sand
the shifting
increasingly wet sand
the sow smiles lewdly trampling
over bluish silvery fish and jellyfish
cast up by the waves which a few moments before
withdrawing their frothy backs
beneath the sun
brought to light this gigantic animal
yes it is a sow as big as a sailing ship
I know for sure its name is Olivia
I'm writing without punctuation in dreams there are no commas
I'm sad I can't be bothered with anything or anybody
I shouldn't have written to her
I shouldn't have written
script rhymes more and more with crypt

I shouldn't have written to her, or else, if I can't help but write to her, if I can't control myself, I should be more careful about the words I send her by e-mail, I tap the keys of the *ordinateur* nonchalantly, as if they weren't mine. The same warning would also apply to her . . . They are our words; we are responsible for them. We don't copy them from a book, they're not other people's words, they're not quotations. Although words like these must have been spoken or written who knows how many times, how could it be otherwise? The danger is that everything becomes fiction, both on the one side and on the other. And in the name of fiction it is possible to say a lot of things. Nothing stops you. You can't see the other person's face, her reaction to your words. Over the telephone at least you can hear her voice, you recognise it, you know you're not alone and you take it into account. The *ordinateur* isn't a good means of communication. It's perverse. In the old days a letter laid down a certain amount of responsibility, and not just stylistically: you wrote it by hand, you thought a little about every sentence beforehand, in order not to be forced to start another letter, to cross out what you'd written and write it all over again, or even to tear up the page and throw it in the bin. The *ordinateur*, precisely because it allows you to make corrections with ease, prevents you from thinking seriously, it pushes you into a kind of disresponsibilisation; I don't know exactly what to call it.

You've got plenty of time to change it, you tell yourself. You promise yourself that you'll rewrite it. Indeed, you have all the time in the world. In the end . . . But you don't do it. You're lazy. And Pastenague (or who?) presses the key to dispatch the e-mail into thin air. Afterwards, you regret it, but it's too late.

If only that were all! . . .

But to play the intellectual, the writer with philosophical and sociological reading, I was possessed to write to her in my e-mails the 'chasm between generations' and other stuff that led me unwittingly on to the idea of old age. A sensitive subject for me and ultimately for her too, especially if it's going to turn into a leitmotiv.

I also wanted to talk to you about the 'generation gap,' which to some is almost a chasm, but not to you or to Bourdieu. But what about to me? Being schizophrenic, I have bridged it with the help of

Pastenague and I haven't had to ask myself all the questions raised by Dufour, who, in his latest book, comes across as an anti-capitalist, but also a conservative.

You came back at me with little piggies and I realise that I'm ridiculous. I fell into a trap. Pastenague is away; I don't know where he's roaming. I look in the mirror and I am slightly afraid: my left ear is on the right side of the mirror, and the right ear on the left . . .

And who am I?

I'm still writing a novel I haven't got around to telling you about; rather, I've decided to destroy the greater part of what I'd written, the result will be something chaotic and hysterical, perhaps not even Paul or John will be brave enough to publish it. But I have to while away the time with something when you aren't here. I think that this is the reason I'm writing you so many e-mails. I admit it: I can't stop myself. I don't have sufficient will.

That I miss you is putting it mildly (as you would say), I have a lump in my throat, I barely manage to feed myself. Don't laugh, but I can feel myself turning into an anorexic. And besides, I'm old . . .

I don't know what I was trying to say with the little piggies . . .

In any event, I shouldn't have moaned about old age, shouldn't have forced her to contradict me and at the same time to think about it. Hasn't Milena realised that I'm old? And if by some miracle she hasn't noticed it for herself, the age difference, that is, what advantage is there in my pointing it out to her? She is still going to realise in the end. But why should I hasten things?

Let's say that at first it was a whim on her part: let's see what that old writer (or 'Romanian writer') is like in bed. She was pleasantly surprised, she wanted to continue, especially since it was quite simple: she was divorced and didn't have to answer to anybody. Marianne was in New York, etc. After her trip to her hometown (is she really in Bratislava?) she might put an end to this affair that began by chance, if not as a game, but then why does she assure me of exactly the opposite, why does she tell me that she can hardly wait to see me in Prague?

A little exaggeration is natural, even necessary, in an amorous relationship. If in life humour is the politeness of desperation, in love exaggeration is also connected with politeness. Unless what is at stake is an authentic sentiment, let's say love. And how could it be . . . My exaggerated words pushed her into exaggerating too. Although chronologically, she was the one who started the bidding at the auction: I miss you! And then she insists that I come to see her in Prague. In Prague, not Bratislava . . .

As far as I'm concerned, not only haven't I distorted the age difference between us, but I have even played it up, with a kind of bitter sarcasm, whenever the opportunity arose. I'm probably older than her father, whom she talks about lovingly, touchingly. Maybe I'm not much younger than her grandfather, who is on his deathbed, as she wrote in an e-mail. This is why she's delaying our seeing each other again. Or maybe, for her reputation, it would also be dangerous if she were to be seen with me in Prague too and to be forced to explain to her acquaintances the nature of the relationship between us. It's still best in Paris, where you blend unnoticed among the millions of inhabitants and tourists. Although in this instance she is exaggerating . . . She's hardly a minor and she has, thank God, passed the fateful age, fateful at least for Balzac, when a woman starts to grow old (now I'm exaggerating in the opposite direction).

Having had enough of my groans (I'm old! I'm ridiculous!), in her next e-mail Milena gave me a lecture in socio-psychology.

Stop saying you're ridiculous (it's the second time). It makes me sad. What's more, I refuse to accept that you are ridiculous. I think that somebody who is genuinely ridiculous is validated/described as such by the other: it is not an essence in itself, it is sooner a relational concept. (It's somehow like in Sartre: the reifying 'gaze' of the other.) But if in a couple the other does not describe you as such, then you are not ridiculous.

But nonetheless if you feel you are ridiculous without the other having labelled you as such, as happens in many situations, I think that it is in fact a mechanism of projection and protection: you experience ridiculousness as a deviation from a norm (let's say a generic one)—therefore, the other is an institution, in the broadest sense: normality, etc.—you anticipate the verdict of this external eye and you interiorise it. Perhaps this ought to be called something else. The difference between the two might be something similar to the relationship between censorship and self-censorship.

I should add that I have a sharp sense of the ridiculous, especially in the second of these hypostases.

If I have been confusing, forgive me: I was improvising, without method. I feel slightly uneasy and I don't know why.

I have never pondered it seriously until now, but when you wrote to me for the first time I thought that without Pastenague you would be ridiculous. I don't think so. It seems to me wonderful to be able to be vulnerable in front of somebody else. It is a luxury.

I would like us to make love right now.

It is the most bewildering thing that has ever happened to me. I have no explanation for it. But explanations have ceased to interest me.

I read it with my heart in my mouth. Things are getting serious, I said to myself. I got up from the table and began to pace around the room. There were many things to be said regarding her e-mail, but since I didn't know where to start, better I didn't say anything. In other words, better I didn't answer her e-mail. At least not right away. I went to the kitchen to make myself a cup of tea. When I came back, I found another message, or rather three photographs of her, in the attachments: one in Venice, one somewhere in Norway, and the third on the streets of Prague, with her smiling at the person taking the photograph. With the dimple in her cheek and gleaming eyes. They were probably older photographs, which she had found there in Bratislava. But why would she send them if the smile was not meant for me?

I didn't reply right away. I went out to meet the same friend with whom I had had lunch. We drank heavily: red wine, and then, with the coffee, a number of glasses of calvados. My friend kept telling me about something, but I can't remember any of it, I was thinking about Milena, about her theory of the ridiculous.

—You're mind is elsewhere, my friend chided me.

I shrugged.

I went back home and reread her e-mail. I didn't look at the photographs again. But nor did I erase them. I sent her an e-mail.

You're an outstanding advocate! You keep trying to defend your im-

age of me, and in the end you will succeed. And that will be the end of the (moral) luxury you're talking about: you'll turn me into a domineering brute. Maybe this is what you need. I'm joking . . . Half-joking . . .

I saw the photos. You're great! I'll end up like one of those truck drivers who pastes photographs of beautiful women all over his windscreen. A Bulgarian truck driver!

take me with you in your truck begged Daisy
what will you do with your car
I don't know
are you going to leave it here
of course not
well then
I'll send it by train to Belgrade
but I'm not going to Belgrade
and from there to Paris
I'm not going to Paris either
but where are you going
I've no idea
how so
I'm waiting for instructions
from who
I can't tell you in fact I don't know
what do you mean you don't know
there's a voice that comes from above
on the telephone
he doesn't need a telephone
an important person
very important

Ever since my very first days as a newcomer to Paris, I have liked to take the Metro. I don't know what it was that attracted me to it even then. Perhaps the smell . . . Yes, yes, I'm not joking. In those years, the Metro had a particular smell, even a peculiar one. I don't know what to compare it to. True, lately, having modernised, it has lost its smell. Of course, I might also invoke the advantage of speed. Because of the increasingly dense traffic, the bus travels much more slowly, especially at peak times, and sometimes you have to wait for more than ten minutes before one arrives. And so I give up the pleasure of looking out of the bus window, especially given that after so many long years I know the streets and buildings of Paris by heart. When I want to admire them at leisure, I don't take the bus, but rather I walk.

In the Metro I like to look at the people. No, not only the women, although obviously I grant them priority. There are some people who read in the Metro, especially women. The women read, and I watch them.

Yesterday I took the Metro from the station at the end of my street, at the intersection of boulevard Raspail and boulevard Saint-Germain. Reaching the platform, I saw Beatrice. Or did I only think I saw her? She was at the other end of the platform. She didn't see me. Her eyes were fixed on the darkness of the tunnel from which the train had to emerge. She was fascinated by that immense black maw that gaped towards her. She was motionless, waiting . . . I walked towards her. Without hurrying. She was wearing a blue raincoat tied at the waist with a kind of cord and tall boots that came up past her knees, the kind that aren't very fashionable any more. Next to her there was a suitcase or rather a quite large travel bag, also blue. Perhaps I ought to have called out to her, waved, but I was still far away. In that instant the train entered the station. I wanted more than anything to board her carriage, which was at the beginning of the train. It had come to a stop just a metre from the tunnel. I broke into a run. Or at least as much of a run as my age allowed. The signal for the train to depart had already sounded when I jumped inside the carriage. But Beatrice was at the other end. It was she; I hadn't been mistaken. I tried to make my way through the people, to get as close to her as I could. She wasn't looking in my direction. The carriage was crowded; it was difficult for me to advance. Two stations later I had barely reached the middle of the carriage. She was looking out the window, at the darkness of the tunnel. The train entered another station, the Gare de Lyon. Then I called out to her: Beatrice! Beatrice! She looked in my direction; she cannot but have seen me, although she pretended not to recognise me.

She quickly turned her head. She got off at the last moment. The doors then closed immediately. I was left inside the carriage, looking at her.

I fall ill only very seldom. This time I think I have the flu: my nose is running, I'm coughing, and I seem to have a slight fever. I haven't been able to find the thermometer; Marianne probably took it with her to New York. I'm lying sprawled in bed, with the *ordinateur* in my lap; I feel very good.

My little ice floe, I have dreams of lady doctors taking turns at my bedside and they all look like you. Some more so, others less so . . . I don't know what I'm ill with. Or why all these lady doctors want to cure me. I wake up and I can't get back to sleep. I think that the dreams have only a present, but not a future. I am incurable.

Maybe because of the flu I write to her too often. And I show that I'm annoyed at her not replying. I show that I am suspicious too. What is she doing all day . . . Am I really jealous? One day she sent me an e-mail in which, among other things, she came across as uneasy about the age difference between us. Or was she just being ironic? But why, even in jest, does she tease me, why does she emphasise the difference and at the same time refuse to talk about it? But if I think about it: what would there be for us to discuss?

Later I realised that she was indeed embarrassed to be seen with me in public. Because of that she wanted me to come to Prague, not to Bratislava, where she probably knows lots of people. She likes me in bed, but she avoids me on the street . . .

Don't be impatient! I didn't write to you yesterday because I was dashing back and forth in taxis between meetings, and in the evening I had my mop cut . . . I didn't have it cut short, just the fringe, and I asked the hairdresser to give it more volume, to make me look decent.

The result is that now I've got a short, semi-chaotic fringe that makes me look like I'm seventeen or eighteen, anyway, it's not exactly good news for us. But that's the situation. It will grow in by the time you come. In any case, I look funny, if not attractive.

My breasts keep growing.

I miss you.

In my opinion, the only tone appropriate to our e-mail correspondence would be a joking one. And so I do my best. But sometimes the recipient doesn't get the joke, doesn't see it. And then she gets annoyed. What about me? I make out I am more and more jealous. Jokingly and at the same time seriously . . . I don't know why I say I 'make out' I am. Maybe I really am . . .

What you tell me about your breasts disturbs me. Why are they growing like that, out of control and in my absence? Take a photograph of them, scan the photograph and send me it as an attachment.

I kiss your smaller breast . . .

Maybe I was also the one who told her about Olivia, the goddess of love. Who else? She liked the idea. And she sent me—I don't know where she got it—a photograph of an enormous-looking sow. Photographed from very close up. Somewhere on the seashore.

A very good idea! Marianne likes pigs too. But she draws a distinction between le cochon *and* le porc. *Olivia is sooner a* cochon. *In the same way, for example, the time that separates us, but elapses to a good end, is a* cochon. *But time in general is a* porc. *Do you agree? But what shall we name the time we shall spend together, that time which seems, at least to me, to be an allurement proffered by the* PORC FÉROCE, *that nonetheless wonderful time? Help me to put this metaphor of the pigsty on its feet.*

I love you swinishly.

Five minutes later:

I've got it! We'll call it a pig. *That is, the first three letters of* pigeon. *That means globalising the pigsty.*

Milena is not to be outdone, as can be seen from the following e-mail:

There's something I really must tell you! I can't wait any longer. I'm in ecstasy! Believe it or not, but in English there is an expression that goes: Pigs might fly, *in other words, miracles might happen.*

What more could you wish?! Pig-pigeon. It all comes together.

Naturally, the genius who came up with this invention was indisputably you. I was, let's say, a faraway muse, and now I'm merely providing a solid exegesis to ground and legitimise the system translinguistically. It's more than a poetic coincidence; it's manna from heaven. Or the manner of heaven . . .

Isn't it . . . divine?

I didn't react to her e-mail. I didn't share in her textualist enthusiasm. And it was a mistake. Later, I realised how conceited she was. But by then it was too late.

For some time, it has been as if Marianne has vanished into thin air. How can I put it . . . She hasn't manifested herself in any way: either over the telephone or via the *ordinateur*. True, to use the *ordinateur* she is forced to go to a cybercafé or to resort to Laura's machine. Might she have got upset? Laura, I mean . . . She was probably there when we spoke on the telephone, and I said what I said. What I said was no big deal! She could hardly take offence at some slightly off-colour jokes between two spouses who have known each other a lifetime. Likewise, it's quite possible that she didn't overhear our telephone conversation. It's even more likely. In the end, little do I care . . .

The truth is that Laura leaves me cold. A Romanian girl who's made it to New York by some unknown means. There's not much in her head . . . She's Marianne's friend. Very nice! I wonder how and why, because the age difference between them is quite big. What can they have in common? What's their friendship based on?

Ultimately, I am in no way obliged to like all her friends. And nor could I have known that she was there next to the telephone, eavesdropping. And if she was there, my wisecracks could be interpreted differently: I was merely trying to be polite by talking like that. I was granting her importance . . .

Or maybe Marianne was jealous because of Laura. That would take the cake! If she wanted to make out she's jealous, she could find more serious reasons; but to be jealous because of that girl who claims to be a big intellectual just because she has studied somewhere or other in the States and speaks good English . . . In the first place, she's not my type. I prefer blondes. I have always liked blondes . . . Or at least brunettes, like Marianne. Sure, not even Milena . . . I admit it, she has dyed hair, but I don't think her real hair colour is raven-black. True, her skin is dark . . . But at least she has blue eyes. Whereas Laura has dark eyes, as big as onions. Turkish eyes . . . Or Indian eyes . . . I won't say anything else lest I be accused of racism.

'Don't you like Indian women?' asks Pastenague. I can't for the life of me rid him of this insufferable habit of reading over my shoulder as I write . . .

I shrug. When they're young, it's said they are good in bed. Fiery. Even without having read the *Kama Sutra*. It may well be . . . But if they're too young, then I'm too old for them. The chasm between generations! And after the age of thirty, they get fat; they all become balabustas.

How old is this girl?

I'll ask Marianne at the first opportunity. But in the end, I could telephone her, rather than waiting for her to call me.

I look for her telephone number in a notebook (yes, I've forgotten it, in fact I don't think I ever memorised it), I don't find it, I get annoyed, Alain calls me on the phone, he can barely articulate his words, I promise to visit him in the next few days. I forget about Marianne, and about Laura. What a voice he had! Frail, hoarse, as if he were speaking from inside a cupboard . . . If he hadn't said it was Alain, I wouldn't have recognised him.

when they reached Trieste Daisy was still hoping that they would go to Paris together that is why she had sent her automobile on ahead by train there was the option of paying to keep it in the train station car park but in any event that was not her concern at the moment and so towards Tsvetan she was all milk and honey true her gentleness and suppleness were richly rewarded with the rigidity of the Bulgarian organ that ravished her until she almost fainted with pleasure

and one fine morning at the hotel during breakfast Tsvetan who was busy guzzling sausage and cabbage with a pickled pepper for relish stopped masticating and said all of a sudden

I'm going to Alès tomorrow

where are we going

not we are going I am going

where

to Alès to watch a truck race

where is this Alès

north of Nîmes

in France

in France obviously

and what will I do

I don't know

Daisy can't understand what has got into him like this out of the blue she chews her lips and looks up and down for the waiter to ask him for a glass of water and something for a headache but she can't see any waiters they have all vanished and indeed the only people left in the breakfast room of the Svevo Hotel are the two of them it was late all the other guests had risen much earlier they had eaten and they had left they were people with affairs to attend to businessmen

what do you mean you don't know

we can travel together as far as Narbonne after that I'm heading to Nîmes and then Alès understand

not really

well then I'll explain it to you later I've got a map in the truck

I don't understand why I can't come with you

the man made no reply he was guzzling the last piece of sausage and what was left of the pickled pepper and Daisy gazed at him in bewilderment for a few moments she looked around her at the empty tables in the restaurant and saw a girl wearing a pink apron with green checks who had just come in carrying an empty tray and she asked her for a bottle of mineral water

and something for her head

the girl couldn't understand Daisy's second request and so

she turned around smiling and Tsvetan took the opportunity to order a plate of cheese and tomatoes and a coffee

the tomatoes are over there the girl pointed to the long buffet table loaded with all kinds of starters

and something for my head requested Daisy

Tsvetan got up to fetch himself some cheese and tomatoes Daisy quickly came after him she asked him in a spoiled voice

why won't you take me with you to Alès

Tsvetan did not deign to reply Daisy lit a cigarette and greedily inhaled the smoke then exhaled it through her mouth her nose and even her ears

smoking isn't allowed

their problem

the man scratched the back of his neck which was quite broad and he looked closely at Daisy

I'll be meeting my friends I won't have time to see to you

but I won't get in your way I'll sit and wait for you in a café

in a café

yes in a café and if another truck driver nicer than you you know one who looks like Depardieu

like who

haven't you seen the film

what film

no film I was joking

I don't know what got into me . . . I was trying to be subtle, but I went and wrote the e-mail below:

If we think of our relationship as a kind of novel (in progress . . .) and judge it, let's say, according to classic literary criteria, it might be said that in our e-mail correspondence we have moved ahead too quickly. The readers will be dissatisfied . . . Or else they will believe that this narrative constructed from e-mails is nothing but a novella, and, what is worse, a house of cards that will eventually come toppling down. This is what I am most afraid of!

This is why I suggest a pause.

But you might argue the opposite and prove to me that we are in an autobiographical fiction: a literary genre with pretentions to in-

novativeness in the history of narrative and which, in my opinion, is based on placing 'the other' in parenthesis. Don't ask me why, because I can't be bothered to make a demonstration.

But if we make a pause, I am afraid you will forget me . . . Or worse (for me), you will seek to make up for it elsewhere.

Pastenague (cynically or with bravado): Wouldn't it be for the best?

Milena did not bother to contradict me. She preferred to give me another lecture. And she proved that she was cleverer than me. But in any case my previous e-mail was stupid. Especially that remark of Pastenague's. I can't understand why he keeps butting in . . . Agreed, in the beginning I called on him to help, but that doesn't mean he should allow himself to say whatever enters his head. Give him an inch and he takes a mile . . .

Now, having got over the effect of the surprise, I have a gastronomic allegory for you (the last, given that my glosses have been excessive as it is): if I have a chocolate cake in the house, I always prefer to eat the whole thing. I don't think I have ever saved any for the day after: let me enjoy it to the full (this too, I admit, is a valid school of thought). I accept the risk of getting indigestion or regretting that I don't have any cake left and that it would have been better to be more moderate.

But it's no good. We all know gluttony is a sin. Or, as the wise proverb goes, it is better to make more haste, less speed, etc. etc.

Therefore I propose a pause.

Now what do I do? At first I cannot help but note that she thinks of herself as a chocolate cake . . . I could turn it into a joke, but I'm afraid she would get upset. Or maybe the cake she wants to eat as quickly as possible is our relationship? Allegories are slippery, dangerous. Either they convey too much or too little . . . And all because of that imbecilic e-mail of mine. And so I try to make amends. I blame it on Pastenague, who, being younger, seriously believes that it's appropriate to act aloof, to play hard to get, to put the other to the test. And I get the fallout.

Erase my last e-mail, don't take any notice of it, delete it. I was talking nonsense. Two-bit literature. It was Pastenague's idea: with women you have to act tough. Or maybe he was thinking of something else and I took it the wrong way. You know, we communicate . . . telepathically. That's why we sometimes miss the mark and end up at cross-purposes.

I like your comparison with the cake. You know, I'm greedier than you imagine, but the cake is far away . . . Is it far away? No matter, I prefer to think and to talk about a faraway cake than not to speak or write to you at all. Don't be angry . . . We'll see each other in Prague soon. I love you.

I ought to have added that it was not because of me that we delayed seeing each other again. Her grandfather was very ill, in a village in northern Slovakia. She was very close to him, naturally. He raised her. Her parents divorced when she was still an innocent child. She didn't have any literary airs at the time . . . I think it was she who told me that, although I'm not entirely sure. Sometimes I get women mixed up. In any event, that was why she had returned to her native land: to see him one last time. The thing about her publisher was an excuse aimed at me. But then why didn't she tell me from the start? She was embarrassed . . . Or else it is more complicated. She imagined that by telling me about her publisher it would be easier for me to suggest that she drop the whole thing and come to Prague and sleep with me. The sparrow dreams of cornmeal! The sparrow being me, obviously . . .

Beatrice did indeed take the train from the Gare de Lyon with great difficulty she stowed her large blue bag which was rather too big for the luggage rack she hung up her raincoat and sat down by the window in front of a middle-aged man he was bald rosy rather corpulent paunchy even this was the overriding impression he gave because of the button missing from his shirt in the compartment it was hot his fat belly was showing and the hair around his belly button he was breathing loudly looking out of the window and from time to time at Beatrice at her large eyes as dark as pitch

she was bored she remembered that she had a book by Alexandre Dumas in her suitcase she stood up and because it was obvious that it would be even harder for her to take the bag down than it had been to lift it up she asked the man in front of her to be so kind would you mind helping me to

and he laughed for some unknown reason and he rose hulking to his feet Beatrice crouched to make room for the belly which now looked more than respectable she lost her balance and was forced to grab onto his trousers what are you doing miss and he moved back holding the bag she got up apologised rummaged in the bag pulled out the book and the man sat down again thank you

what book are you reading

she showed him the cover of the book he nodded and laughed again she laughed too better we just talk he said my name is Dan and I'm Beatrice said Beatrice

they both got off the train at Toulouse

If only you knew how many e-mails like this one I've written you! . . . Luckily I was able to delete them in time, before sending them. Don't be angry . . . And if you're angry already, let me telephone you tonight or tomorrow . . . Although even over the telephone I'm not much sharper. I need to see the person I'm talking to . . . And so I don't know what's for the best. In any case, send me your telephone number by e-mail.

Kisses.

Probably it wasn't a very good idea to ask for her telephone number. Regrets always arrive too late. They're useless.

I didn't get angry. You succeeded in making me insanely mad. I flew into a rage. My hands were shaking with anger. I started tidying up my desk; I was throwing away pieces of paper at random, after first tearing them to shreds. It's very hard for me too, dealing with this whole story. You're not the only one who doesn't know what to do. In any case, next week I'm going to Prague, to see Grandfather.

Underneath there was a telephone number.

Her going to Prague rather set me to thinking. I thought

she'd said her grandfather lived in a village in Slovakia. If he needed to be taken care of in a hospital, why didn't they take him to Bratislava or some other Slovak city? Why Prague? Are the hospitals there better? Does she know a Czech doctor she can trust? She or the photographer . . . Djokovic. I couldn't help myself; I telephoned her. She herself answered. I didn't recognise her right away. At first I was somewhat in doubt. Hello . . . A tiny hello with the stress on the first syllable. A morose voice. Calm, but somehow sullen. Hello, hello, Milena? It was she, but she didn't feel like talking. I suspected she wasn't alone in the room where the telephone was.

—Are you going to Prague? I blurted out.

She told me her grandfather had been admitted to hospital. All right, I understand, but why in Prague? In fact, I only asked the question in my mind. I remained silent. I tried not to come across as jealous. Although it would have been natural for me to ask her why they hadn't taken him to a hospital in Bratislava. That was why I had telephoned her after all. I didn't dare. I could already sense her getting annoyed . . .

—Are you going to Prague? I repeated like a fool. Can I come too?

She didn't answer.

—I'll write to you, she said and hung up.

When she writes to me over the Internet, she's much friendlier than over the telephone. This was an observation that would be borne out not long thereafter, and with a vengeance. She was also of the same opinion.

It's true, we're a catastrophe on the phone (up until recently I thought that I was the only one to blame . . .), it's somewhere between the comical and the ridiculous.

I've calmed down now, but be so good as never to write stuff like that to me again. I suffer from tachycardia.

And I love you.

The part about tachycardia was something new. In Paris, in bed, she didn't have tachycardia . . .

the truck is now driving through northern Italy down the

motorway that stretches from Trieste as far as Turin and thence to Milan Daisy can't get enough of looking at the landscape cooing in pleasure

what lake is that in the distance

Lake Garda

can't we go closer so that we can get a better look it looks very nice please

it's out of our way we'll waste time

so what if we take a little detour it's no big problem

we'll arrive in Turin an hour later or even more

so what it's not like anybody is expecting us

the hotel

I phoned to book the room there's no point hurrying we can arrive even at midnight

at midnight

yes so what

I'm tired

come on be nice I'm not asking you to go right around the lake

that's all we need

just for a little so we can see what it looks like

it looks like any other lake what do you expect

please

in the end Tsvetan grumbling agreed to turn off the motorway and go nearer the lake

look it's clouding over

it doesn't matter it's like that over every lake because the water evaporates look a flock of swans

they're not swans

yes they are

I don't know what you call them in English

he was right they weren't swans they were seagulls but Daisy didn't care about the zoological truth to her birds in flight above a lake were swans and that was all there was to it

we also pass through Mussolini's village

Tsvetan turned his head but he didn't say anything was it a question or a statement the thing is that he didn't really know where the village was he had heard something about it but because he wasn't interested in the subject he didn't pay any attention and so he had forgotten he couldn't even remember the same Salo or something like that

Mussolini's village he repeated in a completely neutral voice

where he spent his final days before they caught him and hanged him head down

head down repeated Tsvetan although he didn't seem at all impressed

him and his mistress

like Ceausescu

I don't know who this Chowshescoo is . . . is he one of your Bulgarians

at last they reached the lake and the road ran along the shore itself the truck was going much slower than on the motorway which allowed Tsvetan to cast a glance at the lake from time to time too

Daisy was in ecstasy she was speechless at so much beauty she had grown thirsty and she kept trying to fish out the bottle of mineral water that had slipped down somewhere in the cab where she was groping her hand came across a kind of smooth fabric like waterproof cloth obviously it wasn't the plastic of the bottle but then what the hell could it be she continued to grope and then she felt a kind of bird

what's this

what do you think an umbrella

is it yours

no

I like the handle

it's not mine somebody left it in the cab

who

a woman . . . an old woman

older than me asked Daisy

and Tsvetan started laughing because the American woman's allusion brought back to mind the face of the old woman even now he still wondered whether it had really been a woman or what the hell he could picture in his mind the army boots and he remembered the metallic croaking voice more like a man's the headscarf covered or rather cast a shadow over the face and so it was quite hard to tell the moustache that sprouted under the nose sooner bore out the hypothesis that it was nonetheless an elderly woman an old crone not to put too fine a point on it

Daisy smiled proud of her sense of humour and kept twisting the umbrella around and it accidentally touched one of the dials of the truck which was going at quite a low but constant speed Tsvetan lost his temper

be careful what are you doing roared the driver

I'm sorry said Daisy frightened

put the damned umbrella away it's not as if it's raining

it was his turn to smile pleased at his own joke then he grabbed the umbrella and flung it behind the seat from where Daisy had taken it shortly before she made no protest nor did she have any cause to but she got up kneeled on the seat to look through the window that separated the cab from the rest of the truck

what are you transporting in those crates in the back

Tsvetan didn't answer right away he turned the steering wheel with a sweeping motion to take a bend

is it contraband asked Daisy

you guessed it

Dan Tesson ran a bistro or rather a bar in Toulouse not far from the station he invited her for a meal Beatrice ordered duck with mushrooms truffles to be precise a local specialty and a cake with almond cream and lemon it was called fenetra

you have good food here

that's right we have a cook who's brimming with talent

by that evening he had hired her it wasn't clear if she would only be a waitress or if she had other jobs on top of that luckily she found out quite quickly but before anything else he forced her to get a tattoo above her belly button and to do that she had to agree to shave off her pubic hair which reached that far up

it's stupid it'll just grow back

never mind we'll shave it off again

although he was getting on in years and had thitherto slept with a flock of women that was the very expression he used Dan lost control when faced with her tits which had in the meantime grown a little but were still firm

he thrust his head between her legs and stayed there for long minutes it wasn't unpleasant but after a while she would have liked something else besides she stroked his bald head the nape of his neck his shoulders she couldn't reach any lower she gripped his head as tightly as she could between her thighs and she could feel his jaws working in time with his tongue he was panting I hope he doesn't suffocate damn it hey that's enough come up here between my tits he was large fat he heaved his belly awkwardly and he was mumbling it wasn't clear what was wrong with him his mouth was slobbery and finally he ventured to glue it to one of her nipples sucked then glued it to the other they changed position she gripped his schlong then his balls cupped them in her hand he had a whacking great schlong but quite flaccid the woman did everything that needed to be done but in vain the man couldn't penetrate her true Beatrice was expecting it Dan got terribly angry and turned brutal then she contracted even more turn on your back but still in vain

and so a few days later he gave her the sack

It's pouring with rain here. After I read your e-mail, I masturbated looking at your photographs. A total failure. I think even a truck driver (be he even Bulgarian) has more imagination. I need the reality, your body: to smell it, to touch it, to cry out: yes! I'm a brute . . .

I sent Milena some pages from the novel and, among other things, she said there were too many women in it.

In fact, not too many women, but too much sex. And too . . . circumstantial. I'm to blame, because I'm thinking less about the novel and more about something else . . .

Initially, I wanted to structure it around the outline for a novel, inciting the reader to construct his own novel. In the light of this idea, the Beatrice character is too heavy-handed. Too forced. It's obvious even now that she will encounter 'the Bulgarian truck' and fall victim to it. A road accident? I am also tempted to give it a tragi-comic ending: the Bulgarian picks her up in his truck and in the cab she finds the umbrella, she fiddles with it, she presses a button . . . Tsvetan stuffs her in one of the crates he has to deliver to Toulouse . . . Why Toulouse? Better Italy.

This narrative thread came up at one point. I didn't have time to start writing it. But I can't use it; there's also Daisy. First I would have to get rid of her. Maybe Milena was right in her e-mail: there are too many women. And she hasn't even read the whole thing yet, I haven't sent her everything I've written, and of what I have sent her, I'm not sure I'm going to keep everything.

I admit that I haven't been brave enough to 'write' a genuine *building site*: to gather the building materials, to lay the narrative bricks and structuring ideas one next to the other, and to let the reader make his own novel. It's true: I have written it, so to speak, under his very eyes, he's been witness to my efforts to write yet another book—a superfluous book, as some will be tempted to call it . . .

Turkish wisdom:

'In order to be happy with a woman, you must love her enormously and never try to understand her.'

'In order to be happy with a man, you must always understand him and love him little.'

by the time they reached Turin night had fallen Tsvetan was grumbling that he was tired he didn't want to eat in the restaurant we'll have a cold dinner sent up to the room

they left the truck on the street behind the hotel which was in an outlying district of the city not very frequented and so there wasn't much danger of anything happening to it but you never know

make sure you lock the door

this truck looks more like a van thought Daisy but she kept that sudden impression to herself

the only thing they took with them to the hotel was a quite small valise it was the valise in which Tsvetan stuffed his pyjamas and a bag of toiletries for the morning he had changed his mind he was of a mind to shave Daisy had persuaded him that his stubble was too harsh it prickled terribly it will get softer as it grows in but what about me how am I supposed to put up with it she was right about that

they were shown to their room by a short hunched creature it wasn't an old woman not at all but she stooped she walked in front of them she reached the door of the room turned her head looked at them smiling winsomely she had blue eyes heavily rouged lips

they entered and Tsvetan locked the door turning the key twice

what about when they bring our dinner

all right but they'll just have to knock I'm going to take a bath he added and with his valise he went into the bathroom which was small but of course had a bathtub and

Daisy heard him swearing furiously in Bulgarian she couldn't understand any of it but she rushed to the bathroom Tsvetan was still swearing she went up to the bathtub where frightened by the furious voice of the truck driver there was a little pink piglet that was squealing and trying unsuccessfully to clamber up the side of the tub jump out flee not hear him anymore

stop yelling like that it's only a poor little piglet that hasn't done you any harm

get it out of there

where am I supposed to take it

I don't know I don't care I want to take a bath

Daisy took the piglet in her arms it wasn't squealing anymore just grunting softly it had had a bad fright the poor thing

ring for the maid commanded Tsvetan and started to take off his shirt his vest he started to take off his trousers now he was just in his long johns

what are you doing call reception

Daisy cradling the pig was gazing admiringly at Tsvetan's body at the muscular hairy torso the animal didn't make a sound maybe it was looking too

go on already

so that she could pick up the telephone Daisy gently placed the pig on the scarlet coverlet of the bed then she changed her mind she pulled off the coverlet and put it on the sheet between the pillows

in the bath Tsvetan was singing his head off

the telephone kept ringing but nobody bothered to answer maybe I dialled the wrong number she dialled again but still no answer

she went up to the bathroom door it was ajar she poked her head inside Tsvetan was soaping himself vigorously she took a few steps forward

I phoned but nobody answered

how so

I don't know

the truck driver stood up furious covered in lather because of the hot water his organ had dilated Daisy looked at it greedily

where's the pig

in the bed

what do you mean in the bed are you completely out of your mind

he got out of the tub and moved menacingly towards her his schlong was swinging from side to side the woman didn't take fright she even threw her arms around him and dragged him towards her pressed herself against him

Alain claims he feels better. I don't know, but he does seem to have put on a little weight. Although he's still just skin and bones, he no longer looks like a skeleton. I found him eating: slowly, with effort. At the beginning of the meal, he explained, it hurts quite badly, but the pain then gradually dies away or else he gets used to it. In passing he told me something rather disquieting: from time to time, without any apparent reason, he's struck by a pain in his ears, which takes a long time to pass. He has started taking a morphine-based medicine. The word morphine has a grim connotation in my mind. All the time I was there, we talked almost entirely about his illness, which was probably natural. I brought him a book about utopia, a subject he used to be passionately interested in. He didn't seem very enthusiastic about it.

We left the building together at around five o'clock in the afternoon. He was going to pick Tristan up from school. The lad will turn eight in a few days time.

she went into a café and tried to gather her thoughts she

missed Victor nothing is more painful than to miss somebody who is dead she looked behind her and saw him for real she had reached the small brook at the bottom of the meadow she turned her head smiling and she saw him in the doorway of the house he was smiling and waving at her turn around come back he called and she shook her head and pretended that she was determined to go farther to enter the water which was not at all deep it didn't come higher than her belly button in the end she didn't dare she came to a stop in the bank she bent down she crouched down as if she had found a snail or a hedgehog come back called Victor and she knew very well the waiter had brought her her coffee she asked for a packet of cigarettes she knew we all know that there is no road back

from her handbag she took the photographs she always carried with her look in this one she was not even two or three years old she was sitting on the bed looking steadily at the camera without a trace of a smile either in her eyes or on her lips it was perhaps the photograph that best summed her up you might almost think that her whole life she has striven to resemble that photograph from childhood

would you like anything else

no thank you

the waiter was lingering next to her as if he wanted to look at the photograph too

Without anything happening outwardly, I woke up with the feeling that nothing was how it should be, that everything was a complicated, meaningless tangle of which no good could come and that in general—no matter how stupid it sounds—life is hard to bear. As you can see, I am in an ecclesiastical mood.

Sometimes I would like to fall asleep and never wake up again.

Don't get frightened, I know you don't like my thanatic impulses (and why would you?). Notwithstanding, I am behaving normally, that is, I meet people, I converse, sometimes I write, and so on; I'm not aboulic.

I don't know why I'm telling you all this. It will probably bring you down or get on your nerves. It's stupid. I wish you were here.

Let me conclude by sending you a short oneiric bulletin: I

dreamed of you again. We were both in a white room, and you had turned into smoke . . . By the end of the dream, we were unable to get out of the room anymore.

After I read her e-mail, I lit a cigarette and paced up and down by the *ordinateur*, like a dog chasing its tail . . . I didn't know how to reply to her. One thing was for sure: if we're not together in Prague right at this moment, it's not my fault. So why should she complain? Maybe it's just a pose . . .

I lit another cigarette. When I finished smoking it, I tried to stub it out the way she does, that is, so that the butt or rather the filter remains haughtily upright, but I didn't succeed. Which is to say, I didn't succeed this time; other times I have succeeded. Maybe I didn't succeed because I turned it into a kind of wager: if I lose, it means I won't be going to Prague. I don't know what got into me . . .

You're right . . . It's all very complicated. Nor do I really understand what's happening to you, to us both.

I'm not a realist novelist, I'm no good at psychology, and nor do I make any great efforts in that direction. When I do, it doesn't come off . . .

I'm writing now and as usual I don't take any pleasure in it. I get annoyed, I don't believe in what I'm writing and, since I can't write unless I think I've found something new, it's torture.

But I'm sick of complaining like this, like an old woman . . .

I love you . . . I like being with you, in every possible way: in bed, talking, in Paris, in Prague, anywhere. Let's have a little patience. Be my good lady doctor. When nothing makes sense, we'll cobble together a meaning, however small, however provisory; it's no great matter. You like being with me: isn't that a meaning? I'd like to know when I can come to Prague. At least for a few days. I love you.

Please answer . . .

She didn't answer on the same day. It was like I was being roasted over a slow fire; I could neither write nor read. I went out of the house, but I didn't feel like doing anything; I didn't know where to go. I wasn't in the mood to go for a walk. Besides, I was afraid that while I was out an e-mail from her might arrive. But nor could I just sit glued to the *ordinateur*, periodically checking my inbox. I didn't dare to write or to roam around on Google as I usually do: her e-mail might arrive at any moment. I was being ridiculous. I had to wrench myself out of that state of anguished waiting. I don't have a television set, and so I went to the cinema. I didn't have the patience to watch the film to the end. It was a complicated film. Auteur cinema . . . A male character, like the narrator in a novel, who was climbing some stairs and on each stair he remembered a different scene, all of which probably linked together by the end. With the help of a seductive and rather exhibitionistic woman, who seemed to be the perpetrator of a series of murders, but I couldn't be absolutely sure, because in order to be sure I would have had to watch the film to the end. The first two murders took place on a rather strange building site where they were digging, not to build something, no question of that, but with the rather dubious object of discovering what lay hidden beneath the surface of the street . . .

And what if Mailena has sent me an e-mail? I'm sorry, I of course meant to say Milena . . . I got up and left the cinema. I went back home, lit a cigarette, switched on the *ordinateur*: nothing.

Still waiting for her reply, I eventually told myself that she wasn't going to write. Why? I didn't know why; it just came to me. Maybe something had happened to her. Maybe she had had an accident. Every hour, I checked my inbox on the *ordinateur*. Like a fool . . . As if she would have been able to inform me if something, something really serious, had happened to her. I didn't want to write to her again; I was afraid of irritating her. And what could I have written to her? I clung to that decision tenaciously. The only thing that would have made sense would have been to telephone her in Bratislava. Even if she wasn't there and had genuinely gone to Prague, maybe somebody would answer the telephone and give me some news of her. I didn't telephone.

I admit that I was jealous. Maybe she was with Djokovic, that is, the photographer I met in the Place Saint-Sulpice; I had seen how he couldn't take his eyes off her in the café . . .

She didn't answer till one evening a few days later.

Yes, if love brings/lends a meaning, then there is a meaning. I'm sorry for my last e-mail; I don't know what got into me . . . I think this whole story throws me off kilter. And the more serious it becomes, in the sense of intense, the more it frightens me. To which you can add my morbid, endemic côté. *I just slept fifteen hours; I feel as if I am emerging after a long convalescence. I've lost weight. I don't know what to tell you, I don't know what's for the best . . .*

The image of the lady doctor rather intrigues me. It sounds like the anthropological structure of the female Savior.

I don't know how to explain the stupid optimism with which I read her tardy reply. Or the e-mail I sent her immediately after that: one that was concessive and imbued with hope. I didn't realise that in fact she was looking for an excuse, because it didn't suit her for me to come to Prague. That was the truth, but I refused to accept it.

You say you've lost weight; that's no good: I don't like my lady doctors to be too thin. What intrigues me is that you have started wondering about the meaning of our relationship. In the beginning, I was the one who did that and it infuriated you, but now here you are . . . Maybe it's not a good thing for us to look for a meaning when we're feeling frustrated. That's for starters . . . Nor is it a good thing if the other person isn't there to be able to answer. I'm not saying you're not right. But maybe everything will change when we see each other again. I don't think about anything else. Don't you think about anything else either . . . If you can . . .

I continue to hope that we shall see each other again soon in Prague. I'm waiting for you to give me the go-ahead, so that I can phone to book a flight.

Marianne, on the telephone:

—I see you've given up your favourite animals . . .

—What animals?

—I haven't seen any eagles, for example . . .

It's true: readers don't like it when an author changes and under the pretext of being innovative recasts his style from one book to the next. For most readers, the ideal would be to read the same book over and over again, with the same characters, but with an unfolding plot, like in a television series. But as this isn't possible, they would at least like the author they have got used to, and whom they enjoy, to stick to the same style. Otherwise they feel disappointed, not to mention frustrated, cheated. I'm not claiming that Marianne is one of them. She was just trying to be ironic . . . She went on:

—You'd do well to remove the news items.

In fact she was right.

—You're right, I said. I'd like you to know that I have removed them.

It wasn't true; I hadn't removed all of them.

—And what will I put in their place?

The absolute stupidity of that question brought her up short. We both remained silent. I gave a cough.

—What are you going? Are you still there?

She didn't answer right away. But she hadn't hung up; I could hear her breathing, like a soft whistling, quicker than usual. It was as if she was jogging while holding the telephone.

—I don't feel well.

—But why? What's happened?

I was genuinely worried. But she didn't feel like talking anymore. Her voice had suddenly grown hoarse.

—I'll tell you some other time. I have to go now.

—Why do you have to go? Are you feeling ill?

—I have to go.

She hung up the telephone.

In that moment, I had no way of knowing that it would be the last time I talked to her over the telephone.

a dog was barking at the moon howling lugubriously just as Beatrice was passing the railings of a park she saw the dog tethered by a leash to a kind of goalpost from which carpets were probably hung to have the dust beaten out of them

she stopped

before long two very young men showed up striplings each carried over his shoulder a kind of shovel or spade they weren't wearing shirts just duck trousers they were laughing chortling grinning from ear to ear they nimbly wielded the shovels miming a grotesque duel and right then three more men appeared they were a little older one had a moustache he brandished a pickaxe over his head as if he were going to cast it like a lance in fact it was a display of joy they were merry exuberant the one with the moustache spat in his palms then he jumped up and caught hold of the crossbar and in the same motion he swung upright to do a handstand then he span around with his legs held outstretched once twice the others below were looking up at him they were laughing the dog was barking rattling its chain it was a regular hullaballoo one of them saw Beatrice who was grasping the railings then the others saw her too and waved at her to enter the yard

come in beautiful

Beatrice ran off down the street which of course descended towards the sea or else it was only a lake the water was visible in the distance there were no waves no ripples motionless petrified gleaming

on the shore of the lack there was a truck covered with a green tarpaulin it looked like a military truck

she had fallen asleep in a café where she was waiting not even she knew what for

they set off from Milan at the crack of dawn they left the piglet in the bathtub and sneaked out of the hotel but nobody would have said anything they had paid the night before the truck awaited them gigantic funereal

Tsvetan didn't say a word he set the truck in motion making robotic movements Daisy was tired and depressed she was staring into space but nonetheless somewhere at the bottom of her soul there still glinted a tiny hope like a straw in a dark stable

maybe she could still persuade him that it was absurd to abandon her like some hitchhiker somewhere by the side of the road in Narbonne . . .

what am I going to do in Narbonne

Tsvetan continued to say nothing he stared at the motorway ahead the truck was going faster and faster he unhesitatingly overtook the other trucks as well as the cars they blew their horns indignantly little did he care

I don't know why it should bother you if I came with you I can be of use to you I'll book a room at a hotel I'll pay if you want to eat with me fine if not then I don't mind I'll wait for you in the room you can come back when you like when you're feeling sleepy or when you've got an appetite for me

Tsvetan didn't answer he didn't even look at the woman sitting next to him he was biting his lips but he couldn't make up his mind to say something anything

it's obvious all my talking is getting on his nerves thought Daisy and she decided not to bother him with her nagging her moaning any more it doesn't do any good worse it infuriates him she knew he had a violent temper he was capable of stopping the truck and making her get out and then she'd find herself all alone by the side of the road among the trucks and cars better she keep silent

they were both silent

Daisy was looking at the landscape but obviously she was less enraptured than she was on the shore of Lake Garda in fact she was worried she was desperately searching for the words to persuade him in less than an hour they would cross the border was Narbonne far from the border she still hadn't lost all hope Tsvetan seemed lost in thought he was probably asking himself questions in the end why would it embarrass him so much to take her with him she couldn't understand it the only reasonable explanation would be that in that small town where they were having the truck race she couldn't remember what it was called somebody was waiting for him a woman to be precise

and Daisy suddenly became thirsty she knew that yesterday a bottle of mineral water had slid down somewhere between the two seats in the cab she started to look for it groping with her hand she came across the umbrella she couldn't resist the temptation she pulled it out with the other hand she found the bottle of water after she'd quenched her thirst she looked at the landscape moving past the window it all looked more or less the same and wasn't particularly interesting she wasn't in the mood for landscapes right now she was holding the umbrella in her lap she ran her fingers over the eagle's head of the handle with her fingertips she kept stroking the beak the eyes pressing them from time to time as if they were buttons and indeed one of the eyes really was a button which when she pressed harder released the blade of a dagger that instantly pierced her under the left breast Tsvetan heard her croak he turned his head and he saw her losing consciousness her head lolling to one side and the umbrella planted in her heart

was she dead

he snatched the umbrella away from her he gripped her wrist he shook her a few times what's wrong he tried to take her pulse beneath his thumb he felt nothing he ran his hand over her face over her eyes he stroked her brow her hair but he quickly drew back his hand to grasp the steering wheel once more and managed to avoid a collision what an idiot he cursed between his teeth a car had slowed down suddenly for some reason or the truck had picked up too much speed especially now with the dead body sitting beside him he had to be more careful he slowed down he took hold of Daisy's wrist again she's kicked the bucket Tsvetan said to himself and the expression on his face remained inscrutable but he was obviously thinking of the old woman with the head scarf how could he not think of her although to be honest I'm beginning to doubt whether such a character really existed I mean to say that it's not out of the question that Tsvetan merely invented her like a realist novelist eager for his narrative to be as lifelike as possible

a quarter of an hour later he reached an exit from the motorway a rather narrow road with a freshly ploughed field on either side with no sign of anybody just a scarecrow a little farther down the road he stopped the truck with the wheels on the right entering the edge of the field he got out of the truck he opened the passenger door and dragged the corpse out Daisy seemed heavier now than the evening before in the hotel room when he was flinging her back and forth

he put her over his shoulder and heaved her up onto the back of the truck under the tarpaulin then he climbed up and opened one of the crates and crammed her inside that small makeshift coffin he put the lid back on

if she comes back to life she'll tap at my window Tsvetan

joked to himself

and he started the truck

The situation has deteriorated on the sentimental front. Because of the telephone call . . . I hurt her; she insulted me. She treated me like a petty bourgeois. Why petty? She's proud; I'm too suspicious. After we had talked on the telephone for more than an hour, she informed me that she was breaking off all contact for an unlimited period.

At my age I can't behave like an impetuous teenager. I have only got what I deserved . . . And besides, I'm ashamed. It's of no consolation to me that I have demonstrated (to whom?) that she is perched high up in her own hyperbole. I'm a blithering idiot!

she had dozed off with her coffee in front of her her head in her hands the waiter passed by her in a hurry he was probably grumbling or who knows what he was thinking of he'd been struck by her as soon as she came in and when he brought her her coffee he tried to make conversation but without much success it was clear he liked her

she hadn't slept for more than a few minutes she told herself you couldn't even call such dozing sleep although it was true that she had dreamed it didn't matter that her dream was now quickly fading from her memory all she could remember was a truck on the seashore and some diggers in fact no there were all kinds of bodies not necessarily human ones that were swarming over the sand in an improvised ballet

in fact she was mistaken that was what she dreamed another time a while ago they were snatches of dream that kept recurring obsessively and so it was of no importance in what order she had dreamed them all kinds of animals that were moving slowly as if filmed in slow motion animals not necessarily terrifying at first she'd been afraid afterwards she got used to it she was no longer fearful of all the things she was seeing

but she was repulsed by the frogs that were hopping around her I don't know how they had come to be in the café where Beatrice was waiting not even she knew very well what she was waiting for or whom

she took a sip of coffee and realised that it had gone cold it meant that she'd nonetheless been asleep for at least ten minutes if not a quarter of an hour she smiled in the direction of the waiter who was looking at her intently and little did she care that a frog had crawled onto his toecap

her eyes were heavy her eyelids were drooping the smile of the waiter

out of breath she reached the truck that was covered with a green tarpaulin from which he unexpectedly emerged they leaped like gigantic frogs they were perhaps soldiers in green uniforms Beatrice broke into a run once more in front of her yawned the black hole of a tunnel like in the Metro but much larger she could still hear behind her the tramping of boots but softer and softer then fading away completely silence she continued to run into the darkness maybe the tunnel led somewhere opened onto the light and probably that word influenced the image because as she was thinking it the darkness seemed to diminish far off but not very far off there was visible an eyelash of light an eye of light which was waxing and Beatrice ran with renewed strength she ran towards the eye of light which was now turning into a mouth gaping wide the luminous grin of the world beyond

the waiter also had other customers to serve what are you up to why are you standing there like a statue said one of the other waiters elbowing him as he passed

How many days has it been since she last wrote to me? I've lost count . . . Against my better judgement, I wrote to her again.

It took me a while to understand what was happening to us. Perhaps also because of you. Because of your hyperbolic style, which I wasn't accustomed to. True, it was also you who helped me understand. Probably unintentionally . . . At one point, realising that we spend more time apart than together, I hinted (without sufficient conviction?) at my desire to turn the situation around, in other words that I should come to Prague or Bratislava—I don't care which—and that we should spend more time, if not together, then at least closer to each other. I clearly saw that this prospect was not to your liking, that it even disturbed you . . .

What you want in fact is a sporadic and clandestine liaison.

The explanation is simple. But I didn't understand it in the beginning. That was how accustomed I had become to taking the blame. You convinced me that I was incapable of 'managing' our relationship. And it's true: I'm not very capable. When I realised that to me my relationship with you was not merely an affair, I no longer knew what to do. But what about you? What was it to you? Are you capable of managing it? I asked myself this question rather late. It wasn't until lately that I realised what was going on in your mind. You do not, you cannot, take responsibility for our relationship. Because of this you prefer it to be clandestine. You don't dare to tell anybody about the relationship between us: neither relatives nor friends. (By the way, how is the photographer from Place Saint-Sulpice?) You don't dare because in fact you're afraid that nobody would accept this 'generational leap' (I don't know what else I can call it). And you may well be right!

It's not a question of jealousy. Or else jealousy only arises secondarily.

After a number of days of cruel silence, Mailena has deigned to reply. She doesn't want us to argue. She'll inform me when I can come to Prague. And so I have to have a little patience. And till then we should both give each other a margin of freedom. She closes ironically with the famous advice handed down to us by the Romans: *carpe diem!*

To this I answered simply:

Carpe diem it is then, but as long as we know . . .

This allusion, which is meant to be funny, will only be understood by Romanian readers. But so what! Aren't I writing for them? And not just for a short time either . . . I write and I wait, with patience comparable to that of Budai-Deleanu, I wait for them to read my work . . .

Alain is having an operation next week for cancer of the bladder. 'It's not a metastasis!' he says, fostering the illusion for his own sake. But right away he adds: 'Je m'en vais en petits morceaux . . .' In such cases, the interlocutor has to come across, if not as optimistic (optimism might be regarded as a slightly frivolous attitude), then at least as ready to contradict the patient's pessimism: a pessimism nonetheless shot through with hope. As if the manifestation of this secondary cancer were not enough, Alain also had a minor heart attack. I'm not sure what this might be or how one finds out.

The accident was spectacular. It happened yesterday afternoon shortly before two o'clock on national road no. 4, between Sézanne and Goguin. The two trucks were unable to avoid the collision. The drivers were injured. One of them was taken to the hospital in Lyngres, the other to the hospital in Sézanne. Fortunately, no other vehicles were involved in the accident. The consequences could have been even more dramatic if another vehicle had crashed into one of the two trucks that collided in the middle of the road. According to the first assessments, it seems that the two trucks were travelling in the same direction, towards the Italian border. One of them, with a Croatian licence plate, was just pulling out of a car park at the side of the road. The other truck, with a Bulgarian licence plate, crashed into it from behind, before turning over. The impact tore off the whole left side of the truck. Crates containing wooden furniture were strewn all over the road. The cab of the Croatian truck was wrecked. It was transporting new cars. One of the cars ended up mangled in a ditch. The other cars were also badly damaged and will have to be scrapped.

The exact causes of the accident are not yet known. The Gendarmerie has begun an investigation.

(L'Ardennais, 23 August 2010)

I have just received an e-mail from Laura. Very brief, like a telegraph.

Marianne in hospital. Condition serious.

Laura

I can't understand what could have happened ... Up to now the treatment seemed to be going well. And in any case the illness she had was completely bizarre, one rarely mentioned in the medical encyclopaedias, but not life-threatening, or at least so the doctors claimed: only two similar cases have ever been recorded in the modern literature, once in the nineteenth century and once in the twentieth. I don't know how to describe it in medical terms. Put simply, Marianne suffers alterations in height; she keeps growing or shrinking. To be more precise, it has happened to her twice since she reached adulthood and since I have known her. Obviously, I don't count growth regarded as normal, which commences at birth and ends at around the age of twenty or twenty-one. The American doctors were very interested in her case and even treated her free of charge. In France, there was a certain amount of interest up to a given point: true, we were both younger (so many years have passed since then!), they told us that it wasn't a serious disease, that is, even some kind of trickery on our part couldn't be ruled out, or rather on my part, because I . . . you know what I mean . . . And nor would it be any wonder when it came to me, a writer of pink elephants.

—There is such a thing as midgets in this world, said the doctor. How am I to obtain proof that she used to be taller than she is now?

—All you have to do is come to our house and look at the marks made in pencil on the bedroom wall . . .

Dr d'Auriol burst out laughing.

A few years passed and things were getting better: Marianne had grown; she had regained her normal height. You couldn't say she was a tall woman, nor could she be considered a midget. I had almost forgotten what had happened to her then, when she had shrunk to the height of a girl at primary school. In any case, my French publisher had forbidden me to write about her illness. 'Enough already,' he'd say. 'Stop feeling sorry for yourself!' But it continued to prey on her mind. I can understand that . . . In the bathroom we had some scales and, I admit, sometimes I used to weigh myself when I thought I was getting too fat. Marianne used to weigh herself every day. At one point, in addition to the scales there also appeared a kind of measuring frame. I didn't say anything. It will pass . . . It's natural that she keep checking her body, especially after the illness, which we were not even sure had passed, and which had left only a few traces. And so I wasn't alarmed. But one fine day, when I came home, I found her in tears: for some time the illness, how can

I put it? the illness had gone into reverse. Instead of shrinking, like the first time, Marianne had begun to grow. At least so she claimed. And after a few months of daily measurements I too became convinced of her suspicion.

—It's nothing, I consoled her, you'll be you like were in your youth again; you'll be taller.

—I'll be taller than you . . .

—Anything's possible. Lately I've been getting shorter, smaller. I'm almost five centimetres shorter than I was as a young man.

—Five centimetres doesn't count. It's normal . . . It happens to everybody in their old age.

—Normal it may be, but it doesn't give me any pleasure . . .

—With me it isn't normal . . . If I keep growing like this, I won't be able to fit in the bed anymore. As it is, I already sleep hunched up, in the trigger position . . .

—The what position?

—The foetal position, if you prefer.

And having been in tears, now she burst out laughing. A nervous laugh, as they say . . . And I laughed too. What did you expect me to do?

—You'll be ashamed to go outside with me, she added. People will turn their heads to stare at us. How will you like that? Go on: tell me! I can picture you now, going off to Maramureș again or God knows where and with whom . . . You'll look for a woman your own height.

Marianne is cheerful and ironic by nature. Even when worried about her illness, she couldn't resist cracking jokes. Especially jokes at my expense. This is what she has always done: she has ironised me, she has, how to say, made fun of me. But I was the closest target . . . I mean, the nearest at hand. The nearest to tongue . . . I didn't go off to Maramureș; she went off to New York. Her friend Laura put out feelers among the doctors over there, who immediately agreed to see her and even treat her free of charge. Scientific curiosity triumphed.

Please keep me up to date. If need be, I'll come over there.

What else could I reply to Laura . . .

A news item in small print in all the morning newspapers:

Icelandic volcano Eyjafjöll began to erupt a few days ago. Lava is spouting to a height of almost eight kilometres above sea level. A dense cloud of ash has formed at the altitude of flight paths. Air traffic has been grounded since yesterday, as the ash endangers aircraft engines. As a precaution, airports have closed throughout Europe. Forced to wait, thousands of passengers are growing desperate.

It's obvious that under the circumstances I'm not going to be able to go to New York. Nor to Prague. Of course, I could always take the train to Prague. But first Mailena will have to make her mind up, get over her annoyance, real or feigned, and then deign to invite me.

not even she knows where she is going or why she is gliding like a doll on rollers the string was pulling her farther and farther south she took the train she hitchhiked when she could she got into a truck that was willing to stop for her and sometimes the intentions of the driver who stopped weren't exactly honourable but she felt like laughing little did she care she was even happy when one of the truck drivers there were two but only one succeeded the other tried too but without success and so one of them after repeated attempts managed to penetrate her and finally Beatrice had the orgasm she'd been craving for so long it hadn't happened to her for quite a while the man was very proud of his accomplishment especially given that the other one

she would have continued to travel with them but the driver who'd been left empty-handed protested banging the steering wheel with his fist true they didn't have much room I'll climb in the back said Beatrice you can't do that said the one who obviously felt slighted have another try she told him or rather his co-driver who'd have been happy to take the girl with them but he couldn't have forced the other one to break the rules even if he had wanted to

they were Belgians probably Belgians from Flanders

they dropped her off not far from a largish village which luckily also had a run-down railway station she boarded a goods train no other trains ran through she found an open door and inside a few boxes and empty wicker baskets she rested her head on one of them and slept like a log she woke up in the station at Narbonne and from there she took the train to Alès because she'd heard that there was going to be a truck race there

why shouldn't we mention that she rather liked truck drivers

Poor readers! I really ought to put in a few full stops here and there, if not even a comma or two . . .

Mailena might reproach me for making use of her e-mails (a part of them) without asking her permission, in order to write a novel (I don't know whether that's the most appropriate word). She might reproach me for turning her into a character: a character, so to say, born from real-life e-mails . . .

But she has no reason to get upset: in the novel (or whatever it might be . . .) I don't give her real name. And so it isn't that serious. In addition, Mailena's e-mails don't look like the e-mails of a writer. That's what I liked about them: the offhandedness with which she wrote them. It was intentional, obviously . . .

And I strive to plagiarise her offhand style, albeit avoiding the abbreviations and spelling mistakes.

Do I make use of her e-mails? So what if I do? It's a question of 'borrowing for higher purposes,' as Thomas Mann used to say, who engaged in the same practice with equanimity.

when Tsvetan reached Alès the races had already begun a few hours ago and he left his truck at the edge of the small town on a side street behind a petrol station he wasn't really allowed to park there but who would be bothering to enforce the regulations everybody was at the races including the police the roads were closed to traffic of course in any case the only way he could have got to the race track was on foot everywhere it was crowded and festive a Turkish truck was in the lead the trucks had come from all kinds of countries he also came across two Romanians chattering among themselves they had dropped out of the race for some reason or else they hadn't even entered it Tsvetan knew a few words of Romanian but too few to be able to understand what they were talking about true he didn't have any intention of competing it was the first time he'd attended such an event he was there out of curiosity and of course he was hoping to meet his friends other truck drivers some of them might even be competing

One morning she telephoned me to tell me that she didn't have an *ordinateur* in Prague nor did she have time to go to a cybercafé (she hadn't seen any, although there must be some somewhere, in the end she would find one . . .). But she had bought a mobile telephone and already sent me two text messages, to which I hadn't reacted. 'What do you mean I didn't react?' I said, trying to hold up against the verbal onslaught. And so I have no right to complain. And she hung up. I lost my temper. I sat down in front of the *ordinateur*, my mouth gaping from floor to ceiling. I wrote her a harsh, cutting, uncompromising e-mail. A real outburst, although towards the end I softened my tone. I accused her of lies and hypocrisy. After that I regretted it, but by then it was too late. The e-mail had flown off at lightning speed to her country, to Prague to be precise. She'll not read it right away, since she claims not to have an *ordinateur*, first she'll have to go to a cybercafé . . .

A lie is humiliating: both for the person doing the lying and the person being lied to. All the more so a badly constructed lie. And your lie about the text messages not being able to get to France isn't one of the world's most successful lies. You didn't send me any text messages. That's the truth. Please don't try to send this afternoon the messages that are supposed not to have got here yesterday, because they are dated: the date and the time. Nor was the lie about your battery running out a stroke of genius. A mobile doesn't just die suddenly. Like the relationship between us, its death throes are prolonged.

Pastenague, who likes to think himself cynical and subtle, says: Fine, but sometimes a lie is necessary. For example, the doctor confronted with an incurable patient, overwhelmed by compassion, is forced to lie. The incurable patient would be I . . . And you are my

sensuous and compassionate lady doctor. Less and less compassionate, that is. There is a Kafka short story, The Country Doctor, *in which the doctor wakes up in bed with the patient. Or rather the other way around . . .*

I won't hide from you that, rather than barefaced lies, I would prefer a friendly cynicism that would allow both of us to make less of an effort; true, there would also be less tension and therefore less passion, and that's probably what you like. But passion entails risks; it feeds on dangers. And, in fact, it's very tiring.

At one point you proposed that we make a kind of pact: each should give the other a margin of freedom. Ultimately, you were asking me not to oblige you to lie. But the way you put it was hypocritical. You didn't tell me: My life, the same as yours, is necessarily double; don't force me to lie . . . On a number of occasions, including today, you assured me that you would never lie to me (not even by omission . . .). But this is way too much, way too hypocritical.

I like to make love to you and probably you do too to me. Between us there is intellectual complicity and reciprocal admiration. Isn't that enough?

When Marianne first noticed that she was getting shorter, she didn't tell me right away. She didn't say anything. And when she did tell me, I couldn't believe it at first: I had never heard of such a phenomenon before. I had read about it, but that was literature rather than reality. At the literary level, I have no cause for complaint, because I can say it allowed me to write two novels and finish the trilogy that began with *Hotel Europa*. Readers (like the doctors?) probably thought it was a metaphor. Some of them. Others were annoyed by it and tossed the book aside. Most of them . . . A metaphor it may be, but we also want to know, they said. Or at least I imagine they did. I can't even know what is going on in my characters' minds with any degree of precision, let alone my readers'. I for one made an effort to describe Marianne's illness in the voice of a realist writer living with the phenomenon day after day and seeing with his own eyes everything that was happening to his own wife. And I think I had quite a lot of patience; I filled up dozens and dozens of pages, without haste, with perseverance, in order to make my story as credible as possible. I waited for the reader to become accustomed to what he was reading. Might I have waited too long? Marianne had already shrunk to the height of a little girl by the time we decided to go to the doctor. But I might be mistaken. Maybe readers were not indignant, maybe they didn't say anything, they had got used to things like that in today's literature, where some characters even turn into beetles. I have heard that in one novel, the narrator turns into a sow. Despite that, the book in question sold tens of thousands of copies.

And so there was no point in my letting it be understood at the end of the novel that in fact it had all been just a dream . . . An uninspired idea! All the more uninspired given that now I can't console them by suggesting it, either her or the readers. You can't take the jug to the same stream twice without it breaking (twice or thrice?). What I mean is that it would become nothing more than a device, which nobody would believe anymore. This may be modern or postmodern literature, or oneiric or whatever you want to call it, but let's not go over the top: as soon as something bizarre, absurd or unpleasant happens, you declare a dream state: hang on, don't be frightened, it's only a dream. Death too is a dream . . . In fact it's the other way around, Marianne, life is a dream, when you die, you wake up. In the latter case, the extreme case, I'm not the one to blame if this means of consolation has come to be a stereotype. Nor am I to blame if I'm forced to go on writing in the twenty-first century. I would have preferred to write in the seventeenth century or, even more so, in the eighteenth century, I swear . . .

When you die, do you wake up? And then what do you do? Do you start all over again? Do you start to dream once more? Such an eventuality is not to my liking at all: to wake up in the ground, in a coffin. For believers, for Christians who believe in resurrection, it must be terrible. I imagine that is how the idea of hell arose. In any case, the idea of resurrection was comforting. And in the modern age, death-like states, when they were able to be ascertained, also had a strong influence on believers, as well as on unbelievers, who were terrified at the thought of being buried alive. Of course, without air you can't last long: you die yet again, that is, you die once and for all. But those few minutes spent in the ground are a true hell. It scares me to think that there is only a hell. Not a heaven too . . .

Laura has given no sign, even though I asked her to keep me up to date. She hasn't sent me a single e-mail. I sent her one, but she didn't reply. Mailena likewise. I have been abandoned within the pages of a novel that seems to me increasingly obscure. But through which I am forced to pass, like through a tunnel . . .

In Egyptian mythology, the story of Isis and Osiris is rather complicated. In order to expound his theory, Ricardou was obviously forced to simplify it.

Isis was the sister of Osiris and at one point she became his wife. Seth, another sibling, killed Osiris out of jealousy. Depressing family goings-on. And so I'll skip over some of the details. To make sure that he would not couple with Isis and have descendants, Seth cut Osiris into fourteen pieces and tossed them in the Nile. Why fourteen and not sixteen? I have no idea . . . With perseverance, Isis looked everywhere, finding him piece by piece. In the end she found only thirteen pieces, as the penis had been swallowed by a fish, which also had a name, I forget what. Isis therefore reconstructed the body and made another penis out of clay. Maybe even a bigger one. But what would have been the point of a bigger one, if it was inert? With the help of Nephtys, who was her sister or maybe a cousin, Isis embalmed the corpse and, thanks to the magic she commanded, she breathed life into it. Not for long, however. But long enough for Osiris to be able to impregnate her, beneath the fascinated eyes of Nephtys.

Why am I relating all these things? So as to emphasise, in the light of Ricardou's theory, that in order to reconstruct the meaning and make it viable, a whole body is required. And the reader's patience, of course . . .

In fact it's more complicated than that. Having entered Greek mythology with the name Artemis, Isis became the goddess of nature. The Greeks covered her with veils, which immediately aroused the curiosity of the thinkers and the poets.

'I am that which was, which is and which will be. No mortal has unveiled me' (inscription from Sais). Gradually, over the centuries, Isis ceased to be the allegorical personification of Nature and became the symbol of universal being. Her veils no longer hide the secrets of Nature, but the mysteries of existence. Existence itself is incomprehensible or at best ineffable. In vain has science progressed . . . It hasn't succeeded in preventing the angst that settles like a mist over and around those who attempt to think.

Alain is home again after the operation. Not only does he live with the prospect of imminent death, but also he is physically tortured by the pain in his throat. I didn't understand much of it. In the place where he was operated, a sac has formed, into which drain all kinds of secretions, whose original course has been disturbed, rerouted as a result of the operation. The doctors are groping in the dark when it comes to his illness. It's hard for them too, he told me. How are you supposed to behave towards a patient who gets angry when you conceal the truth from him but at the same time clings to the slightest hope? I'm talking about the doctors, but the same goes for the patient's friends. Gradually, such a patient grows distant from his friends; he slides towards that moment when he will feel more and more alone. And it's not necessarily the fault of the friends, who don't really know how to behave; nor is it the patient's fault, whose behaviour seems to become more and more selfish, which I find only natural. The patient is so obsessed with his illness and therefore with himself that he is no longer available to others. The friend—unless it be somebody who is also obsessed with himself, such as Edgar R., who is older and even more ill—realises that he must agree to play almost the role of the confessor. Precisely because he feels his existence is threatened, in the relationship the patient needs to exist more than the other.

the Turkish truck driver didn't win the race which was unfair because he was in the lead most of the time and he would have deserved to win he was unlucky a German won after midnight the Turk fell asleep at the wheel and his co-driver couldn't avoid the accident the truck was doing more than two hundred kilometres an hour the driver fell asleep at the exact moment when he ought to have taken a bend next to a park and the truck rammed into the park railings and came to a stop in some very dense elastic bushes the Turks both escaped with their lives but they lost the race that was that they don't have any luck in Europe

Tsvetan didn't go to collect his truck from where he left it the previous day before the race compared with the other trucks as strong and swift as thoroughbred racehorses that had been racing all night his looked less impressive in fact it was a tired old nag with a conked-out engine and increasingly dodgy brakes in Macedonia he had almost collided with Daisy's car because of his brakes which is how he met her afterwards he had noticed a few times that the brakes weren't gripping properly the wheels slid two or three metres before coming to a stop the brakes didn't have enough grip the pads had probably worn down and Tsvetan would be forced to press the pedal to the floor or reduce his speed which wasn't easy or rather impossible if the obstacle appeared unexpectedly

it wasn't prudent to set off on a journey like that

especially since it looked like rain

this is what is going through my mind right now but I don't exactly know what is going through his mind probably not the same thoughts pass through his mind I realise that I know him only superficially I have no idea who he really is this Bulgarian truck driver Marianne was perfectly right to demand to find out details of his life and so I'm looking at him now but anyway it's too late I'll leave him to do whatever he likes I'll see what comes of it afterwards

Tsvetan went into a café for some reason he felt on top form he sat down at a table ordered first a coffee and a jug of water he was thirsty and in any case he always started with water and a coffee he looked around him and didn't see anybody he had met during the race he thought he glimpsed Vasko the Serb but he was at a distance caught up in the crowd and then he lost sight of him he didn't find him again

in a corner of the café he saw Catherine at a table with a

short but very funny girl about Catherine it was said she was a painter and into group sex that's what Bertrand said about her he was a great expert in that kind of thing Tsvetan had met her before he didn't know where exactly maybe in Toulouse or Narbonne at a party Bertrand had introduced him and the painter seemed to be interested in the truck driver are you really Bulgarian she asked and her eyes gleamed unfortunately she had to leave she spoke on her mobile phone she got up and left without saying goodbye she looked angry he stayed hoping she would come back especially after what Bertrand had said about her but Catherine didn't come back

he looked at the two women's table on the off chance that his eyes would meet Catherine's he even made a gesture with his hand raising his open palm towards her but they didn't seem to have seen him or maybe she just didn't remember him obviously how do you expect her to remember but the girl sitting opposite her whom he didn't know seemed to cast a glance at him when she saw his gesture but what could she do Catherine was in the middle of telling her a story she was forced to look at her even if she did cast brief glances at Tsvetan from time to time it was obvious that she was interested she was attracted to that man who looked strong and self-confident and so finally she ventured to touch the hand of the woman in front of her who is that man who keeps waving Catherine looked at Tsvetan who by now had lost all hope of being recognised

I don't know said Catherine

might he be a truck driver

anything is possible

maybe he took part in the race

maybe

don't you know him

I don't know maybe I've met him I've met so many men

I understand

do you like him?

Beatrice nodded her head enthusiastically

well it's very simple said Catherine and vigorously waved her arm at Tsvetan who recovered from the state of apathy that had engulfed him and started to smile but he didn't get up right away

come over here to our table called Catherine raising her voice

I don't know how many days it's been since she wrote to me last. I no longer keep count. One fine morning, I got up, I got dressed, I didn't even have the patience to eat breakfast, I made myself an instant coffee with cold water from the tap, and I gulped it down. Then, I rushed out of the front door, as if I were late. And in fact I was late . . . I should have made this decision long ago: to go to a cybercafé and send myself an e-mail as if it were from her. By now I know very well how to write like her, which is to say, how to imitate her style. Nobody will be able to tell that she wasn't the one who wrote the e-mails. Then, I go back home and send her an e-mail by way of reply. It's no big deal . . .

My grandfather seems to be feeling better. I go to visit him every day. Today he ate some strawberries.

In regard to our relationship, I doubt that it has what might be called a future.

Slightly annoyed, I replied:

We are going through a nebulous period. Entre chien et loup . . . I also detect a communications breakdown between us. I resort to all kinds of dubious artifices. And you are laconic. You don't have the time? Even before, you didn't have the time, but you still made an effort.

Is it the beginning of the end? An end you've orchestrated with great skill? Or does what I think is skill in fact come from a kind of indecisiveness? Intersecting with caprice . . .

Our relationship has no future, you say. In absolute terms, no relationship has a future or, to be precise, it has no perfectly legible future. But ours, you're right, seems moribund. Especially given that you've decided that it's socially impossible. Statistically speaking, it's true. But statistically speaking, our relationship also ought to be doubtful sexually.

Why does the fact that we're both sexually and intellectually compatible (ultimately, we communicate, or rather communicated, at these two levels) not seem to make any impression on you? It made an impression on you in the beginning . . . Back then, you were at pains to persuade me that the 'generation barrier' (which I kept bringing up) was of no importance. The ironic thing is that you managed to persuade me. Too late!

Worse was that we fell into a routine. We became too familiar. Familiar at a distance, nothing can be more damaging to a relationship that has no solid foundations. We lived (at a distance!) God knows how many years in the space of just a few months . . . The characters evolved too quickly, and now they drag themselves onto the stage (at a distance from one another!), they await the denouement, they know that nothing else can happen. They are waiting for the curtain to fall. And I don't know what to invent anymore. What a coup de théâtre . . .

I no longer have the courage to say I love you or to send you my kisses. You have eliminated these words from the repertoire of your e-mails. I get the feeling that I'm alone on the stage. Perhaps this is the truth even . . . I'm alone on the stage and I'm ad-libbing a monologue. Have I forgotten my role? Maybe the play is over and I didn't realise . . .

Alain has died.

No news from Marianne. Laura doesn't make any effort to keep me up to date. I'm uneasy. Even though I don't think the illness she went to New York to treat is life-threatening. But maybe she has something else too; maybe the treatment has triggered some complication or other. She has an extremely rare, almost unknown condition, one that is inconceivable to the minds of European doctors.

I admit that I have been spoiling myself: whenever any doubt arose in my mind about what I was writing, I went running off to Marianne . . . Most of the time she accepted it. She made an effort to read all my scribbles. Now it's clear that she's in a condition that no longer allows her to do so. In fact I don't even know what condition she's in, and Laura doesn't show any sign of life. She couldn't care less about my uneasiness.

I would of course have liked Marianne to read the final part of my text, including the exchange of e-mails with Mailena, but in any event she will read them when the book comes out . . . But what am I to do until then? I need a second pair of eyes before I send the text to my publisher. Alain has died; Paul needs a translation. I telephoned him the other day:

—I've almost finished *The Truck* . . .

—Bravo . . .

He didn't seem very enthusiastic about it. But it would be hard for him to be enthusiastic about every author he publishes!

—Just a few more pages . . .

—Is it something new or more of your stories about gypsies, conmen, art thieves, and Romanians who come to Paris to become rich or famous . . .

—Famous?

—Well, yes . . . Otherwise why do they come to Paris? All right, I'm not saying they always succeed. For that you also need to have other qualities, not just a thirst for glory.

Paris doesn't make anybody famous, I said to myself, and after further small talk we said goodbye and I hung up the telephone.

In what language do Tsvetan and Beatrice speak to each other?

Well, they don't speak to each other . . .

They don't have time to talk.

Yesterday, out of the blue, I bumped into an old friend from university, but with whom I had since fallen out of touch. We went to a café and had the inevitable conversation of two people who haven't seen each other for a long time and want to catch up on what's been happening in each other's lives, for example his third wife had died, but I didn't know whether I should tell him about why Marianne had gone to New York, I hesitated . . .

—But didn't you get divorced?

—No, why should we get divorced?

And so, after we caught up on the essentials, or not as the

case might be, my friend, who I knew was a researcher of eighteenth-century literature, asked:

—Are you still writing or have you given up?

—I'm trying . . . I try to go on.

— . . . because you're not getting any younger. For us it's about time that we bowed out and let the youngsters step up to take our place. Take me, for example: I've retired.

—I'm still trying . . . I'm on the verge of finishing a novel.

—Ah, I'm glad to hear it. I have to admit that I'm not at all au fait with what you write. I read one or two of your early novels. I can't say that I was very enthused. I say this to you in all sincerity. Don't take it amiss . . . Don't be angry . . .

—I'm not angry. Why should I be angry? But I don't write the same as I did . . . in the beginning. I strive to get as close as possible to the reader . . .

—Le grand public . . .

—No, not exactly. I would sooner say . . . le petit public.

—Have you started writing children's literature? pesters the literary researcher, who once published a book about Rousseau and another, if I'm not mistaken, about eighteenth-century love letters or some such thing.

I laughed. What else could I do? In my mind I was very pleased at having bumped into him. Collaring him by his raincoat, I said:

—It was God who made you cross my path . . .

—Or the Devil . . .

—Yes, well, it doesn't matter which. I need somebody who doesn't have any kind of involvement in the text I've written. Would you like to read a few pages? I'm in need of some advice.

—Do you think I'll have the patience?

—Not many pages, but if you don't want to or if you don't have the patience to read the whole novel—in any case it's no longer than two hundred pages—if you can't be bothered, then at least a couple of dozen of pages. An exchange of e-mails and a few comments on an amorous liaison that's gradually fading. Actually, not all that gradually, I'm talking nonsense . . . You'll see.

—Wait a minute, I don't understand: is it a novel made up

of e-mails?

—Not entirely . . .

—You've gone to pot. You've modernised!

—There's no novelty in it. There have been other writers who have made use of e-mails. Women writers in particular. You know that nowadays women writers are . . . In any case, an e-mail is like a letter, perhaps sloppier, but also more spontaneous, more tempestuous, I don't know how to describe it . . .

—I agree, but what I would like to know, because whatever you might say, it's nonetheless highly important . . . *Cette correspondance est-elle réelle ou c'est une fiction?*

And he gave me a waggish look.

What has got into him, with his switching to French like that, I wondered, but I showed neither surprise nor puzzlement. I suspect, in fact I'm more than certain, that it was a quotation. I answered him, also in French:

—*Je ne vois pas de conséquence. Pour dire si un texte est bon ou mauvais, qu'importe de savoir comment on l'a fait.*

And we parted after jotting down each other's telephone number. And e-mail address, of course.

It's all I have left: to write. And not to write to you. You no longer have ears to hear or eyes to read. I hurt you, I wounded your pride, which is enormous: I admit that I haven't read your books and therefore I wasn't able to talk about them. And, of course, I had no inclination to translate them. In the end you realised that for yourself. Your anger has made you deaf. And to avenge yourself, you went blind. You can neither hear nor see me. Now I wait. I have nothing else to do. Although I don't know what I am waiting for. Gradually, because you don't wish either to listen to me or to look at me, you'll forget me. I shall vanish from your eyes: it's the price of freeing myself, of being able to exist outside you. And I shall be able to write for others, not for you. But until then, I must wait and repeat myself, I must keep writing the same things over and over again, which no longer even annoys you, because you don't see them, you take no notice of them.

You're no longer interested in my feelings, or my reproaches, or my stupid jealousy . . .

In the Metro there weren't very many people, there were empty seats, but I didn't feel like sitting down, I remained standing, looking out of the window, I looked at my face reflected in the pane of glass, there was nothing much else to see. A little way away there sat a young and very beautiful woman. Her rather short skirt displayed her legs as far as halfway up her tanned thighs: she had thickish thighs, the way I like them. I look at her for a few moments. Admiringly. How else? She looks back at me and immediately I see her start to stand up and beckon me to take her seat. I vigorously shake my head and for some reason I feel the need to add:

—Thank you, but I'm getting off at the next station.

A stupid thing to say . . . A few seconds later, the Metro enters the next station. I look at the young woman out of the corner of my eye: I see her give an ironic smile. I shrug, visibly annoyed. I turn my head and look elsewhere. I go up to the doors as if I wanted to get off. For an instant I even thought about getting off and then boarding another carriage. But no, I'm not going to do that, I'm an author, not an actor!

What do you want from me? You have decided that I'm old and now you all harass me in the name of politeness or, even worse, pity, pity for one's neighbour. Leave me in peace, I didn't ask you for anything . . . Leave me in peace . . . (to be inserted at the end of the text, in fact I can put it anywhere)

I'm lying in bed and thinking about what Mailena might write to me, what she might reply to my e-mail, now it's obvious that we're not going to gather much moss together. I can't be bothered getting up to go to the cybercafé, which is quite far away. I feel out of sorts. Maybe I'm developing some illness . . . I've a sore throat. Alain had a sore throat too. Even before the operation, not to mention afterwards . . . I'm talking nonsense. . . I'm rambling!

And why, pray tell, should I go to a cybercafé? I can send myself e-mails from her at home too, without leaving the flat, there's no difference, and nobody is going to check who the sender is, literary criticism doesn't deal with questions of that sort. And later on, if I fall into the clutches of the researchers of manuscripts (what manuscripts?), I won't care later on, I'll be dead and buried . . .

Human beings hamper each other when they get tangled up together like trees growing too close together and the light can no longer shine through.

Was that a quotation?

I want to remain free. I need light . . . I don't want you to come to Prague any more.

—It's as if you were afraid . . .

It could only be the voice of Pastenague, but I'm translating so that Romanian citizens whose only foreign language is English will be able to understand it.

—Afraid?!

—Yes, afraid . . .

—Afraid of what?

As usual, Pastenague is sitting somewhere behind me, I can sense him there, although I can't see him. He's invisible, as always . . . When he speaks to me, only I can hear him. But I know for sure that he's the one talking to me, sometimes ironically, sometimes compassionately. Now it's serious. His words conceal anguish, they conceal it and at the same time hint at it.

—I don't know. Afraid to finish, to bring this text to an end, this rambling text, this pointless novel.

—It's not a novel . . .

—Let's see what your publisher has to say, because he is the one who makes the final decision. When I think of the way he has treated me . . .

I pretend not to understand:

—Who?

—Your publisher . . .

—You're exaggerating.

—I learned it from you.

—You learned what from me?

—How to exaggerate . . .

I don't like to talk without being able to see my interlocutor;

this is why I also hate the telephone, I always keep the conversation to a minimum, I'm surly, as if I were always in a bad mood. Nor can I erase or correct my words, which, once the voice has emitted them, reach the other person's ear and work their effect. And I can't attenuate that effect by my facial expression or by a look. It's embarrassing, I know. And so I force myself to keep the conversation as short as possible.

after the night spent with Tsvetan just the two of them in a small hotel in Alès Beatrice was floating in heaven unfortunately there was nobody with whom she could share her euphoria Tsvetan knew only a few words of French and he didn't have the patience to decipher Beatrice's babbling in the language of Shakespeare or rather Bush I beg your pardon I meant Obama and so they communicated mainly by signs which in such moments of exuberance rather irritated Tsvetan which doesn't mean that he didn't like it in bed with her on the contrary he realised right away that he was being put to a test worthy of his manhood her groans of pain were quickly transformed into shouts of pleasure she died and was resurrected and again she died of a pleasure such as she had never experienced until then

she looked out of the window it was a clear sunny morning like in times long ago when at the bottom of the meadow in front of the house there ran a brook in the last few days it had been raining and so the water had risen it was rather higher than usual higher of course than during droughts when the water trickled dry or was barely visible masked by the vegetation which only just held out against the scorching heat it squeezed its way between the rocks and boulders Beatrice would then run down to the brook to look for snails all she found were their shells the snails had already perished from the heat but she gathered them all the same piled them into her little pink basket then she would arrange them by size in her room her parents threw them out every now and then without her noticing or maybe she realised but she liked to collect them from the grass and pick them from among the pebbles more than arranging them on the shelf

with the hedgehogs it was more complicated she would find

them mostly in rainy weather she would look for them endeavouring at the same time to shelter under an umbrella that was much too large for her

you'll catch cold Victor used to say

when Tsvetan came back into the room she was naked in front of the mirror she was lifting her arms standing on tiptoes and stretching as far as she could she gracefully curved her fingers placing her hands together she twisted to the left to the right once twice three times until she grew dizzy she leaned forward she lifted one leg pointing it behind her to maintain her balance of course both arms stretched towards the mirror Beatrice was smiling that she was happy is an understatement

you went to ballet school Tsvetan asked in English

Beatrice grasped the pole with both hands and started to spin around holding on with both arms then with one hand with one leg flexed gracefully and thrust behind her Danet looked pleased although the number was still not ready they had to work on it for a good few more days

now take off your bra

she stopped spinning and took off her bra it wasn't easy she was out of breath

she had breasts like firm pears but later she saw a painting in the Louvre she entered by chance one Sunday afternoon a painting by Titian and indeed the resemblance was striking except that she was somewhat thinner than the woman painted by the Venetian artist different times different attitudes stay as you are Tsvetan's admiration was sincere there was no doubt about that

now we have to set up the guillotine said Danet and two goons came in lugging and pushing a contraption that really did look like a guillotine the blade the boss assured her is made of cardboard you can touch it if you like it isn't dangerous but even so the resemblance was striking the blade gleamed in the beam of the spotlight

here Tsvetan might have asked her whether she was afraid but he said nothing he remained silent and went on looking at her

now with both hands take off your panties that's right very nice arch your back come on a bit more

his voice strong at first would falter as Beatrice took off her bra then her panties in the morning at rehearsals and in the evening he would applaud enthusiastically along with the other customers or drinkers the music would stop and everybody would admire her well-proportioned body and they would all be enchanted astounded by her pelt of thick black hair that sprouted like a squirrel's tail from her fofoloancă

get dressed we're going to Italy said Tsvetan in Bulgarian not even in English

she didn't understand but she did pick up on the word Italy

he helped her to climb into the truck and after hesitating for a few moments he started the engine the brakes sometimes didn't grip the pads were worn down and it was pointless relying on the handbrake because he couldn't use it all the time and in any case not on the motorway

they were soon outside the town leaving behind the last buildings on the outskirts of Alès one- and two-storey houses of a leprous or yellowing white gardens overrun with weeds half-crumbling walls wooden fences slanting as if herds of wild animals had trampled them put to flight by some apparition or other partly domesticated pigs behaving like wild boars

then the plain and hills and farther still on the horizon grey mountains with sparse vegetation she didn't know their name

a monotonous landscape

and so she took from her handbag the box of photographs from which she was never parted her photographs from childhood look in this photograph she can't have been two years old yet a tousled mop of dark hair beneath which the large dark eyes filled the whole of the little face in this one she's walking waddling like a duck yes it's obvious that she's waddling tottering with her arms outstretched trying to find her balance

or here she is sitting on the bed and looking straight into the camera without a trace of a smile either in her eyes or on her lips

she handed the photograph to Tsvetan who looked at it without smiling he shrugged and said in English that people obsessed with their childhood are those who sense that their death is approaching or something like that luckily Beatrice didn't understand much of what he said and nor did I understand everything but I can't be bothered to make him repeat it I wonder whether he knows Russian it would be easier for me

in another photograph she's in the grass not far from the brook Victor photographed her from behind while she was looking for snails or for hedgehogs she was a little older here she was squatting with her arm outstretched

then the guillotine was pushed to the front and she'd kneel with calculated slowness lay her neck on it in the textbook position with both her hands resting on the apparatus that looked terrifyingly like a real guillotine silence would descend all around they would all be holding their breath and she would also be the one who activated a barely visible mechanism and the blade would fall with a dull thud the spectators glasses in hand would shout like at a revolution excited big-time by the rivulets of blood that were trickling on to the floor and even welling into a small red puddle that would soon form a crust coagulate and dry

and she really wasn't afraid

yes she was she was afraid that was why she was walking down the middle of the street with short quick steps it was as dark as if in a forest she trod with quailing heart past lamp posts hunched like branchless leafless trees at first she hurried out of fear she felt like breaking into a run after a while the street abruptly went downhill and at the bottom a kind of valley seemed to open up outlined by the red light of the gibbous impotent sun that was slowly drowning in the sea yes there at the bottom was the sea there could be no doubt about that she was panting barefoot her feet sinking up to the ankles in sand first dry and loose then slightly moist dotted with seaweed from which rose the grinning head of now a lynx now a leopard and a little further on a she-wolf crossed her path but it was only the shadow that pierced her passed through her without flinching the fear had made her reckless for she could not stop now she was forced to keep going to run towards the huge iron gate that loomed threateningly next to the sea the long waves crawled like snakes jostling each other they rolled up the shore struck up against the iron gate with an inscription in Spanish or rather Italian in letters as big as daggers or swords the gate guarded on each side by a lion on which was inscribed something about

she stopped

in other words chuck it all down the toilet although she was next to the sea not merely the water in the bowl and a huge sow washed up like a wave-tossed sailing ship above all have no regrets if you are determined to pass through the gate it was cold and the wind was blowing more and more furiously then it started to rain she hadn't brought her umbrella with her she had a fear of umbrellas

you've been through a lot muttered Tsvetan probably in Bulgarian so you're prepared you needn't be afraid and it seemed to Beatrice that she understood and so it didn't matter which language the truck driver was speaking this business about the languages has started to tire me

in the distance it was pitch black but still she thought to glimpse the outline of grey bodies moving chaotically back and forth probably naked arms reaching out elongating unnaturally in her direction beckoning her as if urging her to come to cross the threshold of the gigantic gate to enter to go among them to join them taking part in that enigmatic ballet

behind there now rose a mountain the colour of burnished brass like a bell whose summit was invisible because it was sliding closer and closer more and more threateningly in any event she no longer hoped to be able to return whence she came

you have no choice urged Tsvetan

with hesitant steps she crossed the threshold of the iron gate

and right away the darkness dissolved the naked bodies in front of her they now turned to an increasingly whitish or pinkish grey they were the same bodies that not long before had been beckoning her desperately but now they no longer paid her any heed they were wielding picks and shovels they were loading sand onto an enormous truck without being able to avoid the seaweed beyond the truck was the sea the waves of the sea that crashed furiously and came to a sudden stop mollified behind the toiling bodies

from time to time they stopped work and called out unintelligible words in a language that sounded Slavic but which and once again the arms stretched out towards her they shoved each other fought each other they all wanted to touch her to clasp her body to grab her to squeeze her to rend her to tear her to pieces but they hampered each other and she began to retreat trying to reach the other side of the imposing arched gate to go back whence she came although she knew that it was not possible it was no longer possible it was no longer possible there was no way back she could already feel the arms the hands the nails which entered her flesh rent her tore away her skin flesh and all

she woke up panting

you were dreaming said Tsvetan you were jerking and talking in your sleep

they were driving through a village of very squat blue yellow and green houses with diminutive inhabitants who were minding their own business which is to say they were hanging clothes on lines they didn't bother to look at that truck speeding down that lane without sidewalks clothes of every colour were dancing gaily in the breeze rosy piglets stole under the clothes on the line racing the ducks it was harder for the hens because they were taller then the truck left the village abruptly entered a forest the road narrowed it was getting narrower and narrower and the light was getting dimmer and dimmer but they could still make out small animals like squirrels although they weren't squirrels they looked more like seahorses they hopped around in front of the truck or made all kinds of leaps flying from one tree to another

naturally the truck was no longer driving over asphalt or even over beaten or muddy earth but over sand in front of him he could no longer see the trees but only water it was a lake or perhaps even the sea the waves were visible through the window which was misted for some reason they were getting higher and higher and it was as if they weren't waves struck by this Beatrice rummaged around agitatedly thrusting her fingers between the two seats in the cab and she naturally came across the umbrella Tsvetan turned on the windscreen wipers and so now they could see clearly the huge snakes that were emerging from the sea they were snakes not waves they were undulating pushing against each other but they did not remain on the shore they returned with a motion lent perfect rhythm probably by the sea currents or by somebody or other lurking far away over the horizon

we're coming up to the tunnel said Tsvetan in Bulgarian and Beatrice realised that at last she understood very well both the language and what was about to happen

NOTES

Page 4

I'll play the part of Flea the Footman to some great writer or other (let's see how they translate that allusion!)

The now proverbial Flea the Footman (Aprodul Purice) was a diminutive page in fifteenth-century Moldavia. During a battle, when Stephen the Great's horse was killed, Flea gave up his own horse, crouching down so that the equally diminutive Stephen could mount using him as a stool.

Page 15

Hodja tore chunks out of himself! (the translator can leave out that last bit, which is in fact a quotation from a brilliant poet who is unknown outside the borders of his native land)

Ion Barbu (1895–1961). Pen name of Dan Barbilian. Major Romanian modernist poet and also brilliant mathematician, for whom 'Barbilian spaces' in geometry are named. The allusion is to the poem 'Nastratin Hogea la Isarlîk' (Nasreddin Hodja at Isarlık), part of Barbu's 'Balkan cycle' of 1921-26, included in the collection *Joc secund* (Secondary Game) (1930). In the poem, the oarless, rudderless bark of the starving Hodja drifts down a river up to the bank where lies the ideal Balkan city of Isarlık. The pasha invites him to partake of the city's plenty, whereupon Hodja commits the act of autophagy alluded to:

Softly the pasha's mellow voice at dusk did die.
Since nor mast nor rope did quiver aboard that ship,
Into every mind tenuous snows began to slip
And oily silences did ooze beneath the sky.

And crisply, like an iron blade that with a sob
Slides into tangled wire mesh to untwine it,
The ice cracked, and over scalp, up spine, it
Resounded around the keen-eared hearkening mob.

Drop by drop, enamel black, on his beard congealed
A brief blood, like two moustaches that branched,

Keen, eternal, in the gums of the cruel haft-grips
His teeth sunken ring-wise in his calf did blanch.

Hodja from his sacred fleshly self his food now rips.

(trans. Alistair Ian Blyth)

Page 127

Ioan Budai-Deleanu (1760–1820)

a writer, philologist and historian, a member of the so-called Transylvanian School, a group of Romanian-speaking writers from Transylavnia, then part of the Austro-Hungarian Empire, who shared Enlightenment and national ideas. His mock-heroic poem *The Tziganiad* (1800) is one of the major works of Romanian literature, but did not become more widely known until more than a century later.

ABOUT THE AUTHOR

Dumitru Tsepeneag is one of the most innovative Romanian writers of the second half of the twentieth century. In 1975, while he was in France, his citizenship was revoked by Ceauşescu, and he was forced into exile. In the 1980s, he started to write in French. He returned to his native language after the Ceauşescu regime ended, but continues to write in his adopted language as well.